# RESPONSE FROM EARLY READERS

## MY MATH CONSULTANTS AND BETA READERS CHIME IN

Few works of fiction truly transport the reader to another place and time, and even fewer give that reader something they can take back home afterwards. 'Geometry Girls' achieves both, breaking down barriers in educational literature and making mathematics not only interesting, but a matter of life and death. **Tom has done his homework ... this work will be a treasure of school libraries everywhere in years to come.**

**Written with a skillful hand** and with the kind of **attention to detail** that will grip an ambitious teenager.

**Young readers will crave more details about the workings of the key solution in each story.**

The MLK story ... an excellent story with a crucially important message for young people in modern Western society. **The mathematics is simple but elegant.**

This was the first time I've seen Bayes' rule used in fiction, let alone in a captivating way! A very enjoyable narrative.

Both the codebreaking and astronomics content are approachable, not too technically heavy.  I especially enjoyed the ending ...

Refreshing .... **there is a special youthful ambition about the whole thing.**

*-- Graham Van Goffrier, third-year PhD candidate (Theoretical neutrino physics)*

Math is not only about formulas and graphs. It's about its applications and illustrations. **Tom has delivered 10 stories which ingeniously weave math into adventure stories.** This intriguing book breaks the glass ceiling which prevents our young female students from pursuing STEM studies.

*--Darshan Maheshwari, Math and Physics Teacher*

We must get girls to enjoy mathematics and to be artists in that field.

We need brilliant minds, women and men, of different social classes, ethnicities and schools of thought ... **We must teach mathematics from different points of view and different perspectives, as Tom has done in this collection of stories.**

*-- Sandra Uve, Author "SuperMujeres, SuperInventoras," from her Foreword*

**'Geography Girls' is a great way to expose young women to real life math that is understandable and fun.** The maths used are simple and can be applied in real world scenarios and shows how important it is to have knowledge of mathematics. Tom's fun approach helps overcome the stigma many young women have about math.

*-- Christopher Urban, Educator*

"Ruby Pi and the Geometry Girls" is one of a collection of must -read stories for readers of all ages who want to **understand the value and some of the magic of mathematics.** Tom's writing will keep you engaged.  To especially those young readers who ask why we study STEM, **get ready for a most surprising read.**

I was not expecting the cipher!!

Teaching is my passion, and story- and game-based education are very near to my heart. Your storytelling is good. The footnotes at the end of the story are very helpful. It is a nice addition.

*-- Aditya Soni, Game developer and Educator*

In this outstanding collection, Tom addresses the chronic problem of our young women dropping out of STEM studies. His stories lend adventure to scientific thinking. These will no doubt stir an interest among readers and encourage them to find the solutions to their daily life problems by using Mathematics.

Tom's stories are challenging, ambitious, and **an excellent resource for developing problem-solving skills.**

"Sasha with the Red Hair" is thoughtful and surprising, like all Tom's stories. **Exceptional ... a family drama disguised as an adventure.**

*-- Tanzeela Siddique, Math Teacher*

Tom, I love your project and I want to be part of it!

I love reading math problems with rich and interesting stories behind them, and this is definitely the extreme version of it!

Tom's stories are colorful, surprising and thrilling!! I could not stop reading until the mysteries were solved !! Rupa and her sister heroines are true role-models who face pulp-fiction dilemmas and solve them ... by applying math!! **An inspiration for all young women interested in STEM.**

History, drama and math make for an exciting adventure ...

Tom communicates a love for math.

*-- Tommaso Pettinari, Physicist, Code developer*

"Ruby Pi and the Mystery of the Old Carthusian" is a tale of a young mathematician who uncovers the truths of the past, layer by layer, using probability and mathematical encoding. She leads the way in uncovering  corruption.

It is an unusual adventure which takes surprising turns. I was pleased to find the irony. **I have never read anything quite like it. As a teacher, I believe it is vital to keep our girls engaged with STEM. We need more of my students to become civil engineers like Rupa.**

*– Pakeeza Sharafat, Teacher*

# GEOMETRY $\pi$ GIRLS

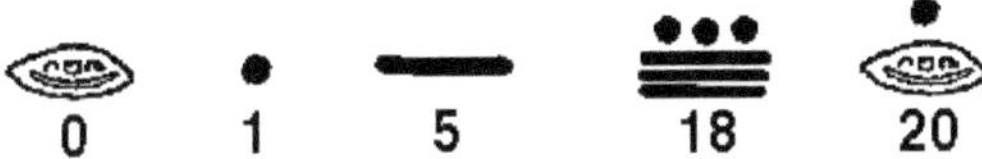


# Credits




ISBNs 978-1-952520-27-3 (paperback )
978-1-952520-28-0 (ebook)


Cover illustration by Iva Dukic.

Pen and Ink illustrations pages 1, 31, 49, 81 copyright 2022 Mai Nguyen. Original commissions for "Ruby Pi."

Diagram tensile strength page 5, geometric pattern page 54, Benin map detail, page 60, photo of MLK and Rustin page 123: Wikimedia Commons.

MLK pendant page 103 by Benjamin Kelley.

Illustration of Chinese girl page 127 by Lorenzo Natale, commissioned for Tom Durwood's "The Illustrated Colonials," Copyright 2019 Lorenzo Natale.

Empire Studies Press

# FIVE ADVENTURES

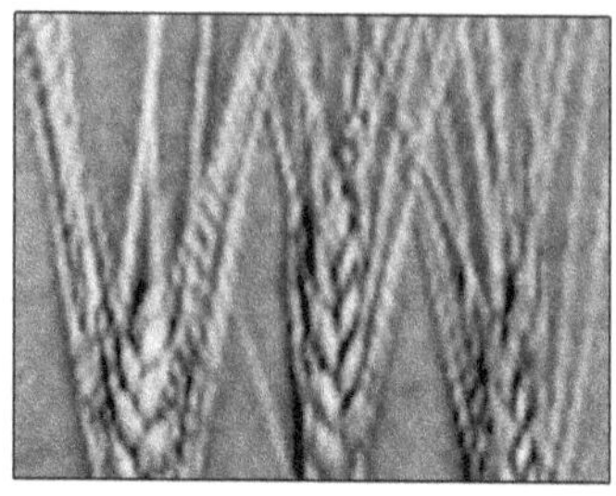

# Contents

A young Indian engineering student in Victorian London uncovers a thirty-year old schoolboy pact.
*Crumbling cathedrals hide a buried mystery*


Teen nurses encounter the most powerful tank ever built at a field hospital in rural France.  The Battle of Montcornet (May 17, 1940) begins.
*A Candy Striper squares off with a Konigstiger tank*


Young Isoke and her brothers attend the Igue festival, intent on buying a bull calf for their village. They bravely thwart an assassination attempt on Queen Nala. The Queen makes Isoke a gift of books, and the consequences change Benin history.
*Geometry for a Warrior Queen*


In the summer of 1958, farm girl Yan Li joins the mathematics team assembled to implement the Great Leap Forward. What she finds is far from 'great' ...
*Clouds in the Forecast*


An enterprising young economist in Florida of 1967 shows Martin Luther King and Bayard Rustin something to change their way of thinking.
*Regression analysis for equality*

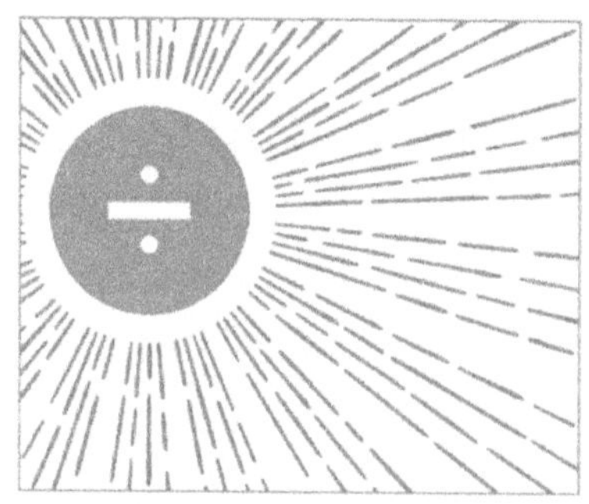



A new survey conducted by Microsoft of 11,500 girls across several countries in Europe found that young girls gain **interest in STEM subjects at age 11 and then lose it again by age 15.** That's a very small window of time to get girls excited about math and science.

-- *Shahrzad Warkentin*

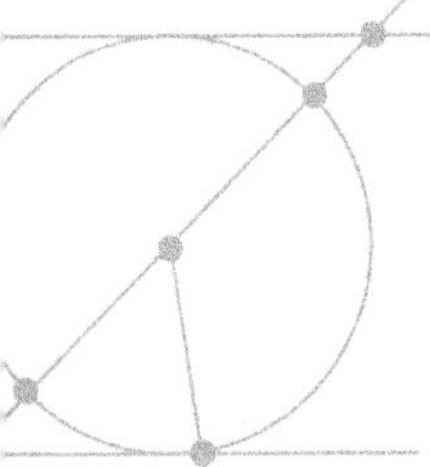

# Foreword

Sandra Uve

Today's science is artistic, expansive and transversal. When we talk about scientific dissemination with a gender perspective, it is important to point out that intersectionality, with its systems of oppression in the face of coexisting identities, does not make any sense either in critical thinking or in the scientific method. We need brilliant minds, women and men, of different social classes, ethnicities and schools of thought, so that the world can continue to evolve. One of the best discoveries of this century, the detection of gravitational waves, was attributed to not just a single person but to many. Science knows no genres, only brilliant ideas that change our lives.

Not only are we clear about that, but science is currently being taught from a broader perspective, showing unlimited capacity. The amalgam of scientific branches, or what we know now under the acronym of STEAM, is a concept that especially motivates girls and teenagers, since it represents a much more flexible possibility when it comes to training, learning and specialization. Almost all the scientists and inventors in my book, however old, were multidisciplinary: from Ada Lovelace to Radia Perlman, who mixed algorithms with music and poetry respectively, to Concha García Monje and Mara Dierssen, who mix robotics and neuroscience with cinema and rock n' roll. The

## We need brilliant minds, women and men, of different social classes, ethnicities and schools of thought ...

possibility of explaining to a girl the story of Mae Jemison and asking her not to stop dancing ballet because it will serve her to be an astronaut, has exponentially enriched my capacity as a science communicator. After years of challenging girls to look at science in a much more generous and creative way, I have been able to see the change in those who are now almost university students: the scientists of the future work from creativity, with all the freedom they have and valuing new stances with regards to possible gender exclusions.

However, of all scientific branches, mathematics is the one which needs the most dissemination with a gender and socio-emotional perspective. Mathematics generates anguish in children from approximately 5 or 6 years old. If you add to that from the age of 7 girls have already discarded mathematics because they are difficult, and socially they have been taught that the most complicated is intended for boys, we have a double challenge when it comes to disseminating and promoting this scientific branch. We must get them to enjoy mathematics and to be artists in that field. We must vindicate the pioneers who are still unknown and do not appear in schoolbooks. We must teach mathematics from different points of view and different perspectives, as Tom has done in this collection of stories, because this is when good creativity is generated and when the brain acts using all its superpowers: observation, curiosity, calculation, analysis, logic, empathy...

But above all we must give them current references in mathematics and put in context the social and future importance they have. Since I started my research for the project "SuperWomen, SuperInventors, SuperScientists" in 2015, life has changed a lot and therefore the needs are different. The world is controlled by experts in mathematics, especially algorithms. There is a very high labor demand that seeks mathematicians and we do not have

> We must get girls to enjoy mathematics and to be artists in that field.

them yet. Jobs are waiting, so we must go the extra mile in disseminating mathematics. And we must do it from childhood and all the way through higher education.  By standardizing mathematics in the classroom, we will ensure equitable and egalitarian training,  so that as much talent as possible, without gender bias, enriches our science and technology system.

*Sandra Uve*
*Illustrator, Writer and Scientist Communicator, Author*
*"SuperMujeres, SuperInventoras. Ideas brillantes que transformaron nuestra vida" Planeta, 2018*
*www.sandrauve.com*
*https://www.instagram.com/sandra_uve_official_account/*

# Author's Welcome

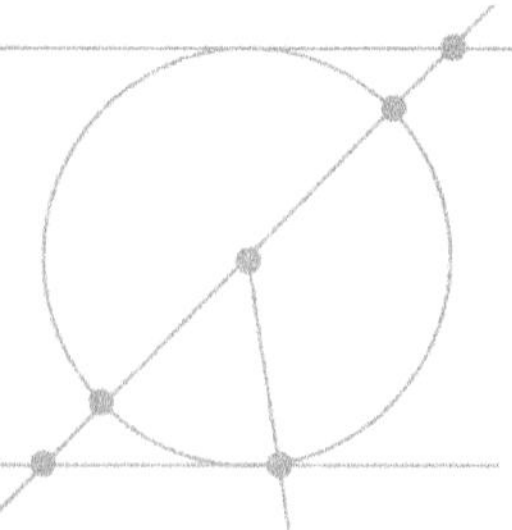

I am an English teacher and history buff. I have no aptitude for math. This makes me the perfect person to write these stories.

In these ten stories, I have tried to come at mathematics from different angles – colorful applications, how concepts and relationships were 'discovered' in historical contexts, placing the calculations in a variety of adventure scenarios.

The phrase "Geometry Girls" comes from the sixth story, "The Architect," when Queen Nala uses it sarcastically (and she pays for that!). It is meant to suggest all areas of applied mathematics.

I intend these stories to be challenging. I use words like 'susseration' and 'solipsistic' in the hope that my readers will look them up. Math is hard, and so is understanding the real significance of the Battle of Montcornet, or architecture in Africa.

I am offering links between you and applied math on my web site, www.themathgirls.com. More free material in this vein is to come.

Second and third collections of stories are also on the way.

A friend of mine used to work in Human Resources at a top tech company. Many, many candidates moved through the office, all badly wanting to work there.

The first meetings often ended with the interviewer saying this:

"I just have one last question before you go:

*How many piano tuners are there in Manhattan?*

Piano tuners, Manhattan – how many, would you say?"

The tech representative, of course, is not looking for a number but for a process.  They want to see how you think.

Here is how your answer might go:

*I'm not sure, but it certainly involves a few basic questions and answers.*

*How many people live in Manhattan? How many households? How many music schools? Music studios and plays on Broadway? How long does it take a piano tuner to tune a single piano? How long does a piano stay in tune?*

On and on, in this vein, and you're hired.

One thing I think is that Mathematics is about problem solving.  I think it is about using careful logic to crack all the codes that surround us, both in the man-made world and the natural world.

One thing I know is that you really, really need to understand both the mechanics of calculation and mathematical thinking in general as a lens to look at the world.

Your pal,

*Tom D.*
*Seattle, WA*

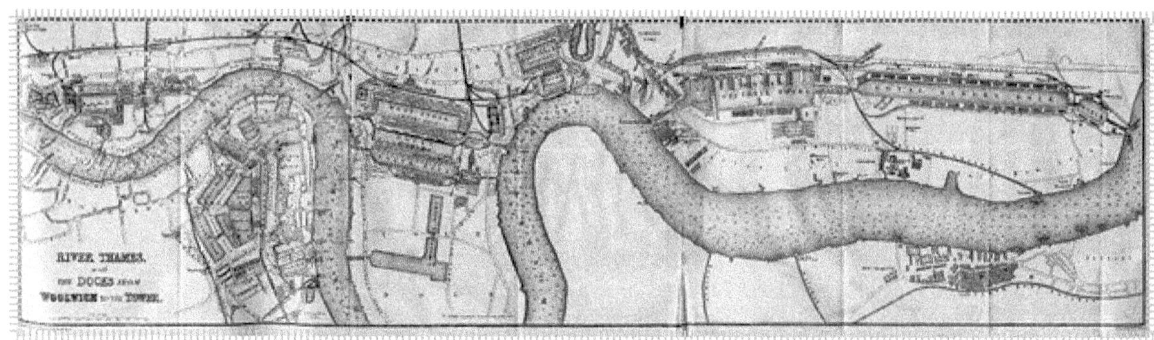



*Port of London*

# Let no-one ignorant of Geometry enter here.

*-- Sign above the entrance to the*

*Greek philosopher Plato's Academy*

# VOLUME 1

**A young engineer stumbles into a deadly mystery from the past.**

## CASE OF THE OLD CARTHUSIANS

**Rising mathematician Rupa P. (nicknamed 'Ruby Pi') wins her engineering firm's bid to repair the cathedral at the Charterhouse School. Deadly accidents beset the project. Rupa discovers that a buried object is behind the sabotage attempts. She must resolve secrets buried in the past – and fight off the corruption in her own office -- to save the day.**

# PROLOGUES: A PACT AMONG SCHOOLBOYS

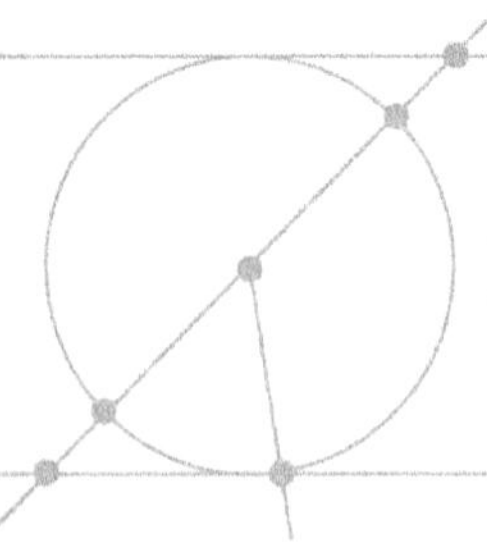

The desire for a controlled world arises from the
inability to honor the unknown.
-- *Xiaowei Wang*

## GODALMING, SURREY (1877)

THE SCHOOLBOYS IN THEIR MULTI-COLORED TIES PLAYED handball against the stone buttresses of the cathedral at Charterhouse School, up the hill from the village of Godalming, in the County of Surrey.

The boys enjoyed making as much noise as possible, to compensate for sitting quietly in class all morning, studying Chaucer ("The Miller's Tale: Comedy or Tragedy?"), Leeuwenhoek, and Gauss's Theorem.

That half-hour between lunch and the bell for afternoon classes was filled with the slamming of rubber balls on stone and scuffling shoes and calls of "In!" and "Foul!"

Eton Fives is a loud and uncommon sport.

The three Sixth formers, the most senior students on campus, stood aside from the fray, smoking cigarettes.

"I have enlisted," announced Nigel, a Duckite.

A handball caromed just over his head.

"What?" cried Borgo, a day student.

"You're really doing it?" asked Gavin, a Daviesite.

"Yes. I shouldn't be here. This school is ridiculous."

"We should all three go!" said Gavin. "They say the Boers are kicking our boys up and down the veldt."

"I can't," said Borgo. "I can't go. My family is counting on me."

In the distance, the Brooke Hall bells rang, signaling afternoon classes.

The trio of friends stubbed out the cigarettes, hid the ashes and butts in tins, and hid the tins in their bookbags.

"There might be a way," ventured Nigel, thoughtfully.

## Transvaal, South Africa (Seven Months Later)

"The two blacks," said the much-hated Sergeant, Preshaw.

The small company of British soldiers huddled beneath the cluster of trees, forlorn figures in the vast grasslands. A stream nearby, a tributary of the Limpopo, gurgled on its way to the sea.

"What about the blacks?" asked Gavin.

His face was smudged, and gaunt, and a dead look had crept into his eyes.

"Kill them," commanded the Sergeant.

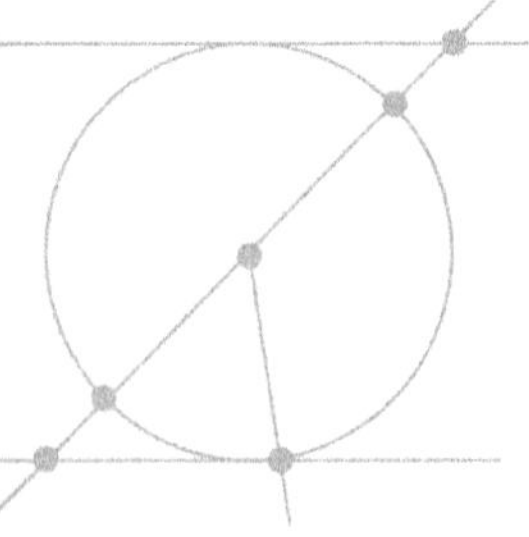

# BROOKE HALL: ENTER RUPA

Build a church so great that those who come after
will deem us mad to have attempted it.
*– Fernando de Contreras*

GODALMING, SURREY (1897)

"YOU CAN TALK ALL YOU WANT," SAID RUPA to the six distinguished gentlemen. "But that entire cathedral will collapse if you don't add 14 tons of load-bearing capacity to those buttresses."

"And blocks of stone," she added, "will not get the job done."

A certain authority in Rupa's voice and bearing belied the girl's sheer youth. The men of Brooke Hall were unused to such direct talk.

The generous dimensions of the teenaged engineer's eyes called attention to the fine structure of her nose and cheeks. A certain humor, a spark, shone in her quick smile. The deep brown and coffee tones of her complexion were sharply offset by the white of her teeth, and the bright collar of her chestnut-dark suit.

Her black hair was pinned in a French bun. A ruby necklace dangled at her neck.

Altogether, Miss Rupashana Lal Pyradhakrishnan lent an exotic presence to the sparse conference room of Brooke Hall, faculty quarters of the Charterhouse School.

The school's cathedral, landmark of the district, two centuries old, needed rehabilitation. A chunk of stone had fallen from the high vaults of one of the flying buttresses which supported the roof. The great buttresses needed to be rebuilt if they were to continue fulfilling their function.

The small London engineering firm of Childress Engineering was the last to bid on the job.

"Surely you are engineering the wrong empire, Miss Chakrabarty," remarked the clever Chemistry Instructor, Allsopp, to Rupa.

"Shouldn't you be building *dams* along the *Irrawaddy*?"

Tall, quiet Vardan, Rupa's escort and cousin, who stood by the doorway, shifted his weight at the comment's racism.

"I am apparently needed here," replied Rupa evenly.

Miss Rupashana Lal Pyradhakrishnan was not equipped with a reverse gear.

She pointed to the blackboard to remind them.

Here is what she had written there:

"Yes yes," said the blond-mopped Mathematician, Simon Veevers. "The tensile strengths. More than sufficient. Good good. All good, but -- "

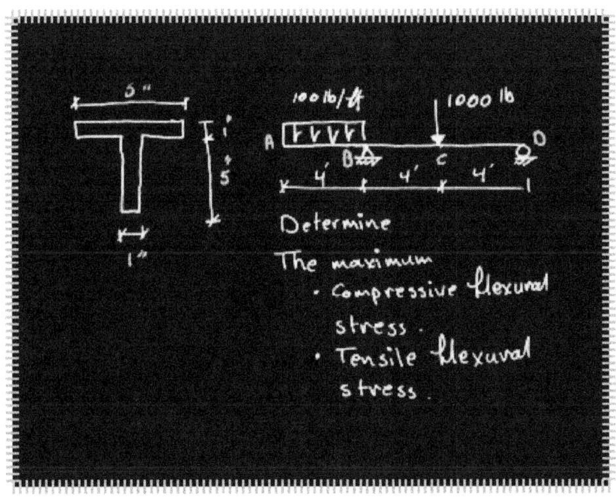


"But are you sure your scheme will work?" asked JCP, the Latin master. "Won't the whole damn thing collapse while you are reinforcing the buttresses? Good God."

"Dankmar Adler and Louis Sullivan seem to think it will work," replied Rupa. "The ten-story Wainwright Building yet stands. So, Yes."

"*Dankmar Adler*," sniffed Allsopp.

"Miss Chakrabarty," chimed in the Literature Instructor, Summerscale. "Of the five firms to bid on this contract, yours is the first to mention these new steels. These new techniques."

"Sir, I assure you that a framework of thin steel rods will support your cathedral a thousand years. You can see by the mathematics. Their tensile strength is most considerable. If the skyscrapers don't convince you, surely the numbers will."

"Innovative, I'm sure," remarked JCP. "The Americans -- '

"The *Americans*? If stone masonry worked for the *Cistercians*.," barked Allsopp impatiently, "I'm sure it will work for -- "

"Thank you." Simon Veevers stood, signaling that the meeting was over.

"It has been most enlightening."

"One more minute, if I may, Simon," interrupted Andrew Childress, the engineering firm's senior partner.

His genteel manner and amiable timbre of voice set everyone at ease. Andrew Childress was OC – Old Carthusian, that is, an alumnus (Weekite) of the school -- and therefore a member of the family.

"There is one other component of our bid," Childress proclaimed, smiling.

Rupa had reached down into the oversized tapestry satchel beneath her chair ... to remove a set of architectural plans. These she now unrolled on the expansive conference table.

"Oh my!" cried Allsopp.

"It's the Racquets Courts!" cried Summerscale, himself a skilled player. "You've re-imagined them! Brilliant!"

"Well, I never -- " said Veevers.

"*Aut viam inveniam faciam*," laughed JCP. "None more than this!"

Rupa unsheathed more designs, sheet after sheet of color renderings of the abandoned-but-still-standing sports venue. She took out and black-and-white elevations and worked-out details, to the appreciative cooing of Brooke Hall's faculty members. JCP used his cane to walk around the large table, so he could read all of the schematics.

"We will throw in these plans as well as site supervision. Same price," stated Andrew Childress.

"You did all these on speculation?" Veevers asked Rupa.

"We want this contract," Rupa replied. She omitted mention of the days she spent searching through the Hall of Records to find the original construction plans.

"We must have this!" declared Summerscale. "The students, the OC's, everyone will love it -- "

Pleased at the fuss over her work, Rupa stepped back from the table.
She glanced at Vardan., who was smiling, proud of his talented cousin.
She twirled the chain of the ruby necklace, as she often did while thinking.

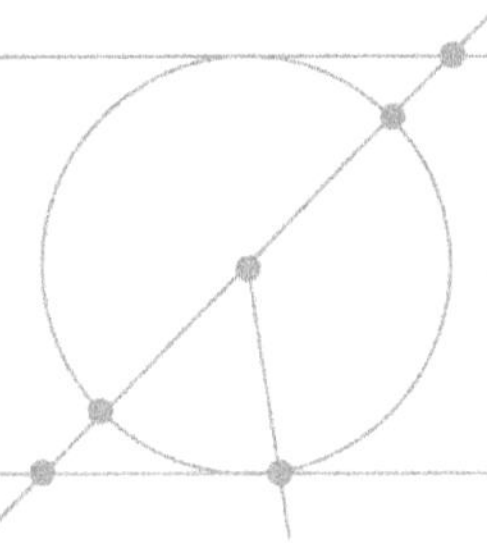

# CONSTRUCTION BEGINS -- INTERRUPTION

Understanding stress distribution from the upper
vaulted nave to the flying buttress system would
contribute greatly to the preservation efforts of
the great cathedrals...
*-- RDY Kim*

EARLY THE FIRST MORNING OF CONSTRUCTION, BEFORE the Surveyors could set up their stations, before the masons began their stonecutting and the cranes their lifting, Rupa gathered her crew under the pin oak on the cathedral lawn.

"It is a fine morning," she said.

"I am glad to start. I am glad to be working with you. Your references speak highly of you, each.

"This is an unusual contract. A complex job. We will draw eyes from all the Commonwealth if we do it correctly.

"And if all goes well, you and I will work together on other jobs.

"Our firm is bidding on two bridges in Luton, a castle in Dornoch, and the new Bank and Monument stations. Including tunnels.

"We are partners, you and I. I need your best ideas. Your best efforts.

"I will never attempt to direct you personally, but rather consult with Master Dent.

"I will work hard to earn your trust. In return, I ask for the same respect you would show any co-worker.

"For many of you, working under the supervision of a Hindu -- a teenaged, female Hindu -- is a new experience."

A breeze ruffled the sheets of canvas draping the scaffolding up the soaring pillars on the cathedral.

"If I hear the word 'dhoby' or 'washerwoman' or 'wog' or 'Paki' or anything remotely derisive, if you glare at me, if you slow-time your efforts, if you do not share with the team your every honest thought as to how to improve this project -- then you will have no place here. It will happen quickly. I carry the list of replacement names with me."

The crew had heard the stories. These Indians, they stuck together. Their network stretched from the Penrhyn Quarries to the Liverpool wharfs. If they blackballed you, your next job might be on a pretty bridge across a frozen swamp in the tundra of Nunavut.

"Very well."

Rupa smoothed out her skirt. She hid her hands in the deep pockets of the skirt.

"My father worked seven years of indenture, stoking coal ovens in the ships of the British merchant marine. So that my family could move from Tirabhukti to London.

"My Mother keeps a jar of pennies on the mantle at my home, saving for my CQE exam.

"I will not let them down."

Rupa glanced over at Vardan, who stood by the tree trunk. The Quiet One blinked, once, as though he were nodding in support.

"We will encounter unexpected obstacles. Many.

"Together, we will meet every challenge.

"Our preparations have been thorough. The numbers have been triple-checked, the stress levels all tested. We can start on both the cathedral and the racquets sites this morning.

"These are enormously heavy stone blocks we are dealing with. Mind the swinging cables overhead at all times. Leave the welders plenty of room.

"We will break at 11:30 for the first-shift lunch, 12:30 for the second shift.

"So. Good luck to us all.

"Mister Dent."

The site chief stepped forward.

They all bowed heads.

Rupa held hands with the supervisor, Dent, on her left and Benson, a stonecutter, on her right. She gripped hard, for her hands had barely stopped shaking.

"Our Father," began Dent, "who art in Heaven, hallowed be thy name.

"Protect your children from the evils of rushing, complacency, pride, deceit, and distraction.

"Give them the vision to see the dangers before them, and the skills to avoid them.

"Grant us the ambition to work hard. Give us the strength to finish what we have started.

"May our hands always be prepared to lighten another's load, and may our hearts do so willingly.

"Without You, we are nothing.

"Amen."

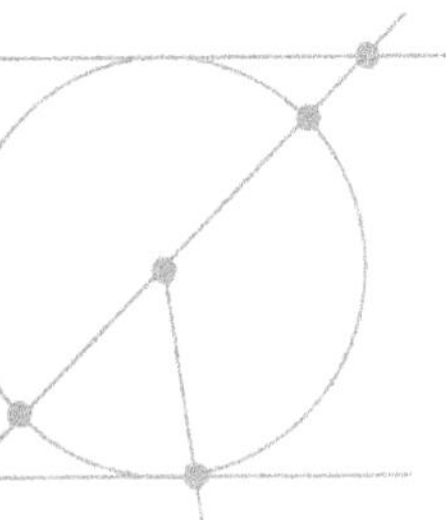

# MIDNIGHT AT DAVIESITES

Words are not the currency I choose .
That is your money.
*-- Fatimah Asghar*

"CATHEDRALS LIKE THIS ONE ARE THE MOST dearly-held of English landmarks," said Rupa's eternal escort, companion, and cousin, Vardan, in the dining room that evening.

A young professional woman – even one as independent as Rupa -- could not criss-cross the districts of the United Kingdom unattended. One never knew which streets were safe, and to attend classes at the Engineering Society at King's College, she had to cross through the wharfs of the Strand.

"It's a small miracle that they gave you that contract," continued Vardan as they ate. "Great God, how can anyone eat this food? What even is it?"

"Retrofitting the old-fashioned way," replied Rupa, "removing those stone vaults one by one, with tower cranes and pulleys, would have cost ten times the price we quoted. Besides, they did not give me any contract, or any moneys. They gave it to Andrew, who is one of them."

Simon Veevers, housemaster at Daviesites, had offered to host the pair during construction. Rupa and Vardan ate at a table separate from the boys, and slept in rooms on the other side of the house than the students.

"We should visit the bank tomorrow morning," remarked Vardan thoughtfully. "Make sure the check clears." He was always suspicious of the empire's inner workings, and always protective of his talented cousin.

"This is corned beef, I think," Rupa concluded, looking at her plate. "The white things are potatoes."

Daviesites sits on a rise overlooking the cathedral and the entire southern edge of the Charterhouse campus. A converted Victorian home, the rambling, friendly white clapboard structure featured tall gabled windows and uneven wooden floors.

Unable to sleep, reviewing her figures by lamplight, Rupa sat in her flannel nightgown at the desk by the window of her little bedroom. A spell of silence filled the night.

*What is that?*

Through the window, she saw figures moving across the silver nightscape.

The figures descended on the cathedral.

Wrapping herself tight in a bathrobe and slippers, Rupa tip-toed down the warped stairs of Daviesites and out across the hushed, moonlit lawns.

The looming shapes of the school structures in the distance might have been contours of war towers, or craggy cliffs, or upland moors, or brooding minarets, in some more ancient time.

A mist shrouded her feet.

She reached the cathedral. She held the lantern high. She could see shovels scattered. Someone had been digging, along the eastern foundations of the cathedral.

A rush came towards her from the shadows to her left.

A glancing blow sent her tumbling into the dewy grass.

Her lantern clattered to the ground and blinked out.

Three running figures raced away from her, east and north, towards the playing fields.

"Hey!" Rupa called.

The shimmering of the stars, or perhaps a dusting in the Sea of Tranquility, a hundred thousand miles above where she stood, made the silver blanket of splendid night blink.

She stared hard into the shadows. Could she see traces of different colors within the black-brown umbrage, streaks of sapphire and jade and ocean-deep blues?

No ghost walked the lawns and classrooms. No phantom, or banshee, or nocturnal demon. No haunted thing stalked those grounds.

But some hidden thing did.

She would find it out.

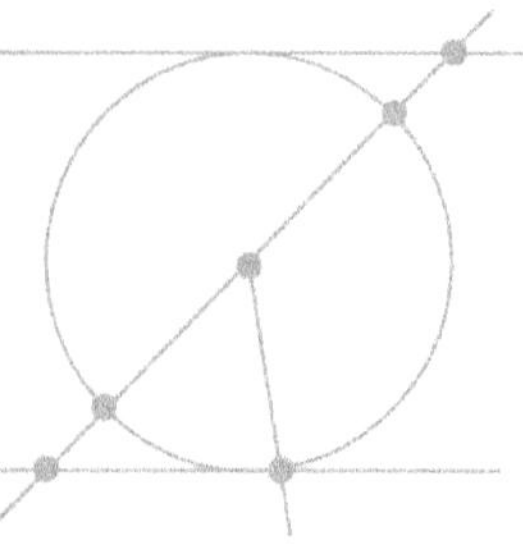

# LAND MINE AND MASON ACCIDENT

Trent wasn't looking for trouble.
It came looking for him.
– *The Mountain Valley War*

T HE MORNING WAS BRIGHT AND BUSY. THE familiar sound of hammers and drills and surveyor's shouts filled the Spring air. Workers removed weeds from the neglected brick-and- stone structure.

The Charterhouse School was reclaiming its racquets courts.

Racquets is an imperial version of squash on oversized, slate-floored courts which display a command of space and dimension as well as English hand-eye skills. The courts are as lengthy as a Cuban Jai Alai *fronton*, as tall as a Basque pelota court.

Twenty years prior, the heavy slate had proven too much for the foundations. The walls tilted and cracked. Local engineers could not get the numbers right, so their attempts to rebuild ended in disaster. The project had lain fallow.

Today, Rupa and her crew began to change all that. Her detailed calculations of elevations and stress requirements would not fail. New pylons were pounded into place, and concrete poured. The resulting pedestal could hold the Taj Mahal.

Cleared of weeds, shrubs and two decades of neglect, the courts held their original, handsome proportions. Teams of workers hammered the pylons deep into the Surrey soil --

"Stop!! Stop!!"

An unexpected voice interrupted the morning work. Running over the knoll, Dent waved his hands vigorously.

His face and voice betrayed real concern.

They followed him back to the cathedral site.

There, by the east wall, unearthed by the workers' shovels, close to the spot where Rupa had seen the phantom diggers the night before, lay exposed to sunlight two white discs.

"What on earth -- ?

The objects looked simple enough, yet somehow deadly in their simplicity. As big as large frying pans, the devices' smooth flat surfaces were made of thin sheet iron. The objects' perimeters were trimmed with jute -- a fuse. The ends of the fuses were protected by brass caps covered with beeswax.

"Land mines," said one of the masons.

"Seen one like that outside Witwatersrand. On the Transvaal.

"The Boers would leave 'em behind. Parting gifts, as they retreated ..."

"Stay back!" shouted one of the school guards, a military man himself.

"The damn thing detonates by direct contact with the friction primer," he warned gravely. "Place an ounce of weight on it and we'll all be blown to the treetops."

"But who -- ?" asked Rupa.

"No one knows," replied Dent.

"Brooke Hall will want a halt on all construction, I'm afraid," said the Mathematician, Veevers, arriving as more guards gathered to gingerly inspect the two land mines. "Until we can get to the bottom of this.

"Is Andrew around? Perhaps he could help -- "

"Of course," said Rupa. "I will send for him."

Just then, Vardan appeared, carrying an envelope.

Rupa opened the envelope.

She read the message from the bank.

"The account is empty," said she, ruefully, once Veevers had stepped away, but Vardan already knew.

# THE INVESTIGATION

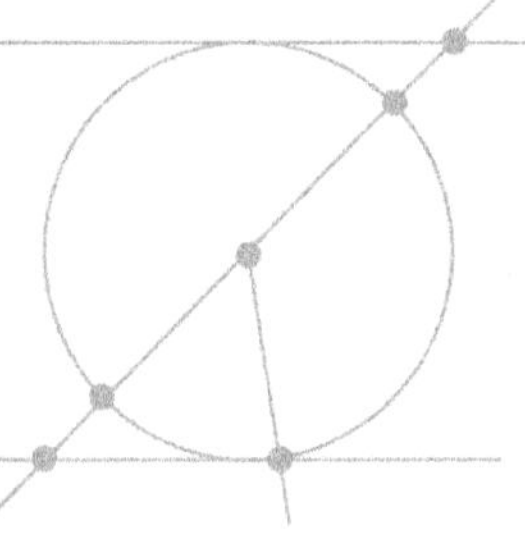

The brick walls are there to stop the people who
don't want it badly enough.
*-- Randy Pausch*

**"I**s this the document you wanted?"** asked Miss Deepa**, a smart, friendly
woman from Bihar, the region adjacent to Tirabhukti (Mithira, that is, ances-
tral home to Rupa's clan).

Rupa leaned out from her perch on the ladder to look.

"Almost," said Rupa.

The two women (and Vardan) searched through the Hall of Records, among files
and shelves and stacks of permits, building codes, wills, marriage licenses, construction permits, lawsuits, judgments, certificates, civil code  violations and paper records
of all kinds from marriage licenses.

"Did your Mother ever tell you where we met?" asked Miss Deepa, Head Librarian,
Mistress of the Hall of Records.

"*The Bengal Princess*," replied Rupa.

The older woman smiled and nodded.

"Your mother saved leftovers and cheese and cookies during the day, so I wouldn't
cry at night."

The Hall of Records was housed in a free-standing tower, a stone structure on the
high ground at the northern end of the Charterhouse School campus. The tower had
originally been built as an observatory of the moon and stars, a competitor to Her-

stmonceux (as far back as that!). The Hall's high ceilings and roomy proportions led upward to a curved ceiling and broad skylight. Blue and gold tiles were still visible in the ceiling, still hoping to capture a bit of astrology.

In 1804, when the River Wey flooded, all of the civic records of the city of Guilford and the Waverly Borough Council were transferred there as well, so the clever clerks of Charterhouse devised a balcony of flat files, moving ladders on racks, and a full second story of shelving.

Buckets of rice and straw hid in corners to take away moisture, the enemy of all things paper.

"Here it is!" declared Rupa, holding up a file. "I knew I had seen it in here the last time ...."

"Now, if we can just make payroll -- "

"Set thy heart upon thy work, but never on its reward," quoted Miss Deepa.

"It's not for me, *Deepaji*. It is my workers who need to be rewarded," replied Rupa. "In the form of a paycheck. On Friday. And today is Wednesday.

"Is Master Andrew up to his tricks again? The gambling?" asked Miss Deepa.

"It looks like it. The bank has placed a hold on our account."

Rupa carefully descended the ladder, file in hand.

"I can help, perhaps," offered Miss Deepa.

There was a delay in Rupa's response. She had noticed another document, and now she scrutinized it, closely, as though looking through the parchment at some water-mark or message in pentimento, buried under the ink's surface.

"Got something!" called Vardan from across the way.

His call bounced off the fixed stars embedded in the colored tile of the Hall of Records ceilings.

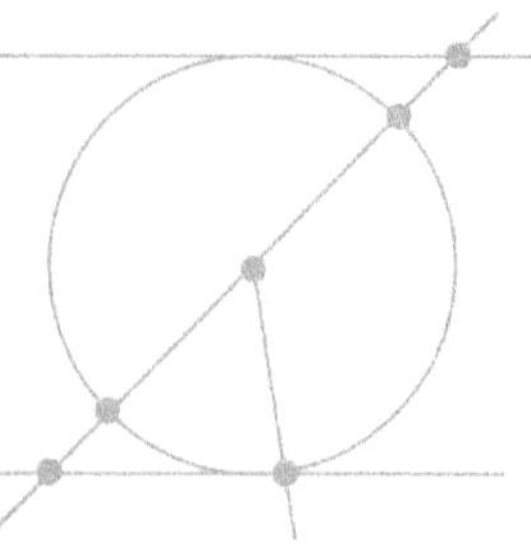

# FULL BOER WAR SCENE

This is all we get.
*– Audrey Niffenegger*

"**K**ILL THEM," REPEATED SERGEANT PRESHAW. "They'll talk. They'll give our position away. When they get home."

"The Boers are the enemy, not the Sotho," replied Gavin angrily.

"You can walk them over there," ordered Preshaw.

This sudden presentation of a sharp moral choice changed everything. Forever.

The Sixth Dragoons (Innskilling) had offered the two Sotho, a slim brother and sister, food in exchange for directions. They were little more than children. The trusting pair stood, waiting patiently, on the path eastward, towards the river.

Gavin Hedley, late of Duckites House of the Charterhouse School in Godalming, Surrey, had no intention of murdering them.

No Carthusian would do such a thing, not even in the upside-down universe of the Boer War.

"We'll come round Majuba ... meet Anstruther at Laing's Nek," said Preshaw.

"Like hell," said Gavin, seething. "You seriously think Anstruther is going to just jump in, after losing a hundred men at Bronkhorstpruit -- "

The others were watching, now. Mutiny is no subtle thing, and it's clear to all when such a line is crossed.

Nigel moved his position, so he might lead the two African children to safety.

"Well, that's the Ninety-fourth's job, innit?" snarled Preshaw, buckling on his gun belt.

"You've lost your mind, Preshaw," warned Gavin. Borgo, now a ragged, hollow-eyed version of the schoolboy he had once been, moved closer to Gavin, to make clear his own loyalties. His own deadly intent.

Gavin Hedley turned to face the Sergeant, hands hovering at his waist.

"This is insubordination -- " cried Preshaw.

"I hereby *relieve you of command!*" declared Gavin. "Someone has to!"

Preshaw snapped.

With a bitter curse, he rushed forward to storm his aristocrat mutineers, pulling out his own pistol – a Mauser C95 – as he did so.

Whether he meant to wave it or fire it in the air, none will know, for young Gavin Hedley let loose –

Borgo blasted three rounds --

Gavin swung his rifle and fired –

Bullets tore at the ground in front of the advancing Preshaw and then climbed up on him, spraying bloody wounds across the legs and torso.

With a grunt of surprise, Sergeant Preshaw fell ...but not before placing a .45 cartridge in Gavin's chest, killing him.

Borgo screamed at this development. He waved his rifle to warn his fellow soldiers to back off, while moving to reach his bloodied friend –

Preshaw breathed his last.

The men of the Sixth Dragoons (Innskilling) rallied, as if waking from a dream.

Borgo was quickly shot dead for his act of mutiny. Now two of the Carthusians lay dead.

Before the regiment could stop him, Nigel swept the two Sotho with him and jumped over the cliff and into the river, which turned out to be a tributary of the Limpopo.

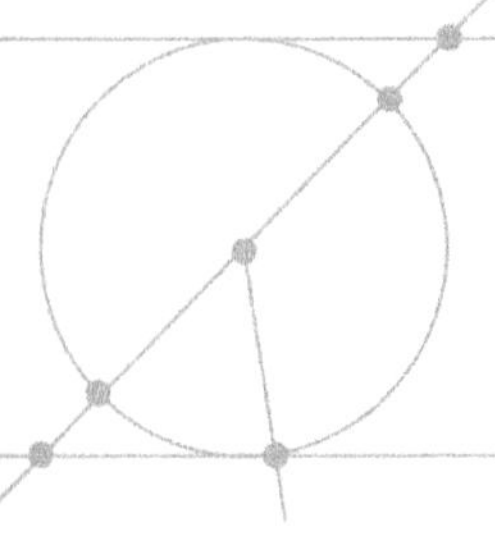

# A PUZZLE SOLVED: BROOKE HALL SCENE #2

I can see where it's all going, now.
*-- Kay Oyegun*

**B**ROOKE HALL WAS DEADLY QUIET SO EARLY in the morning. There was tightly-wound tension in the air, although it was hard to say where it came from. The faculty's faces were grim as they took their seats.

Rupa stood at the conference table.

"Gentlemen. I believe we can re-start the project ," she announced.

"Having lost only the one day."

"What?" cried Simon Veevers, the Mathematician.

"Impossible," exclaimed JCP. "The safety of our students -- "

"But how can that be?" asked Summerscale. "The land-mine s-- "

"The land mines were fakes," said Allsopp, the Chemist.

He had been sitting next to Rupa, and now he stood, in clear alliance with her.

"Unloaded. They are blanks," said Allsopp. "Props in a stage play. Meant to scare us away. There was never any real danger."

"Whoever planted those mines was looking for something that was buried long ago," explained Rupa.

Each face had turned towards her.

"He wanted to stop us from digging so we would not find it first."

"Who -- ?" demanded Veevers.

"But what -- " stammered JCP.

"He was looking for this," said Rupa.

She tossed a flat metal box, such as you might find in a bank deposit slot, onto the table. It clattered as it landed, its lid popping open.

"And what was in it?" cried Summerscale.

"This."

The young woman laid out a document, several pages thick. She smoothed the pages with her hands.

"It's a tontine."

"*A what?*" exclaimed Veevers.

"A *taunting?*" asked Summerscale.

"A tontine,' she continued. "Taun-teen. A lottery-style agreement. A type of investment."

She seemed to have grown in stature.

She seemed to care very much that she was delivering an accurate message, and delivering it clearly. She did not seem to care how it might be received.

"The tontine was a pact among three Charterhouse students. From the year 1877," explained Allsopp, the Chemist. "They left school to fight on the Transvaal. But before they left, they formed a tontine. Last one alive gets the payout."

"Don't you mean Borgo and Hedley," asked JCP, "and that Weekite, what was his name -- "

"Smith. Nigel Smith," replied Allsopp. "Yes. Borgo could not leave school because his family depended on him. His expectations. Future earnings. This way, if he died they would be taken care of.

"The original sum has multiplied. Quite handsomely.

"And these were in the box as well. Letters from Nigel Smith, the last survivor of the tontine, giving the missing narrative. Events in the Transvaal.

"We haven't gone through everything, but it appears that Hedley refused an order to butcher two natives and was killed for showing a conscience. Borgo was shot while coming to his aid. Smith escaped down the Limpopo with the natives. He died a year later, with Walter Long, at Lydenburg."

"Well done," murmured JCP.

Rupa took her seat.

"Then who buried all this lot?" asked JCP, once these revelations had been absorbed by the group.

"Apparently, a member of Borgo's family. They refused the tontine payout, which was rightfully theirs. Called it blood money."

"This is an absurdity!" snorted Veevers, who rose from his chair in protest --

"You don't want to leave," said Allsopp to Veevers.

Two school guards entered.

"Ronald," Summerscale asked Allsopp, "how did you come to find out about all this?"

"Miss Pyradhakrishnan and her companion came to visit me last night. She found a civil court record registering the filing of the tontine. Date and time and attorney.

"We are in her debt." He turned towards her and bowed. "Deeply in her debt."

"And Miss Pyradhakrishnan?" asked Summerscale. "How did you know where it was buried?"

"These markings were on the certificate," she replied.

She displayed this:

# eEreg vveffuvjxh tjlgvv

"That is a highly unusual sequence," Rupa explained. "Letters don't come like that naturally.

"It represents directions. A sort of verbal map. A treasure map. In code."

The decoded message was this:

# Pin oak 20 steps n 7 sTeps w

"We dug it up last night."

"And who was the saboteur?" cried Summerscale.

"The same mathematician who helped Hedley and Borgo write the code," answered Allsopp.

He turned to Veevers.

"Simon had read the tontine. He probably helped draft it. A clause in it calls for a third party providing we are still going through it, but the indication is that, with the letters from Smith and the original document, he could stake a claim to the entire fortune."

"*Vocatus atque non vocatus Deus aderit*," exclaimed JCP (and rightly so).

"Remarkable," commented Summerscale. "Most remarkable. One for the Annals of Empire."

"You can't prove anything," hissed Veevers.

His face had gone flushed and red, his features distorted with hatred.

"I'm afraid we can," retorted Allsopp as the Mathematician was led away.

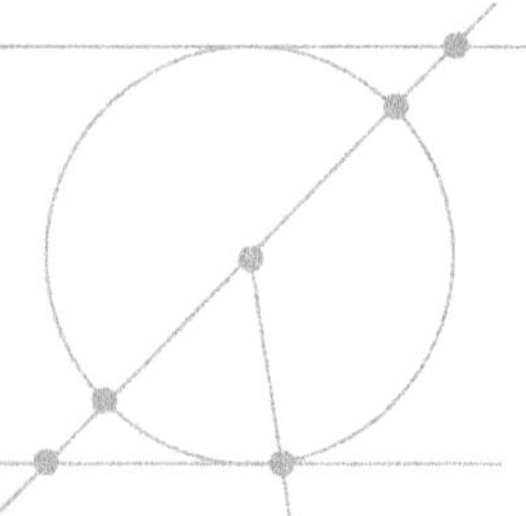

# EPILOGUE

Using algorithms as a mirror to reflect the real
world isn't always helpful.
*-- Hannah Fry*

**P**AYROLL WAS DELIVERED ON TIME.

Miss Deepa had called in her nephew, a clever, scraggly law clerk named Porbandar, who had worked with the Surrey banks on embezzlements. He had been able to open a modest line of credit with this bank's officers, tied to the firm's contract with the renowned school.

Late Friday, on the knoll, up from the cathedral, Rupa's second-in-command, Dent, handed out the wage envelopes.

He shook each man's hand and exchanged a word or two.

Rupa stood and watched, from up the slope, under the oak's branches.

The day's work had gone better than she could have hoped. The pylons had sunk almost exactly according to their estimated depths. The trusses fit snugly. All her tables had held true.

Now the carpenters' tools and glass-tube levels were cleaned and stacked and locked away.

Now two of the surveyors, educated men, smiled at her and nodded as they passed down the line. They had heard all about Rupa's efforts.

Now one of the masons, a burly Welshman, caught Rupa's eye. The mason saluted her.

She smiled and gave a bow.

The last of the workers' wages were paid.

Night was coming.

All of the Carthusians were safe in their chambers, warm light illuminating their textbook stories of Ophelia and Lavoisier's conservation of mass and Queen Elizabeth I ("More sinned against than sinning?").

Thanks to Porbander, the offices of Childress Engineering would open for business Monday with a new, slightly altered signage:

*Childress and Associates, Engineers*

Rupa was the associate to whom the title referred.

A cool breeze ruffled the battened-down canvas sheets across the scaffolds.

The stars would soon come out,

In the Surrey dusk, Associate Engineer Rupalshara Lal Pyradhakrishnan, a Londoner born in the foothills of Tirabhukti, in the province Mithila , twirled the ruby necklace with her slender fingers.

"Let's go," called Vardan. "Or we'll miss the last train."

"Yes," said Rupa. "Yes, Vardaji. We'll start again Monday."

# TOM'S NOTES

O N MY TIMELINE, THE ORIGINAL CONSTRUCTION OF the Charterhouse Cathedral took place in 1806. In reality, the year was 1922.

The scenario with the two Sotho captives derives from the moral choice dilemma of the excellent book (and film) "Lone Survivor," namely: Do you kill prisoners whom you know will betray your position if set free?

In this story, Rupa is using applied mathematics to rebuild the cathedral.

Here is how a real-life mathematician (Ms. Tanzeela Siddique) begins to approach the question of holding up the cathedral roof:

First, she sets out a mission statement:

**In the above problem, we need to find the maximum compressive and tensile stresses of a T-shaped beam.**

Then, she assigns terms:

**In general, the stress in a cross-section is equal to moment 'M' at the point of interest and the distance 'Y' from the neutral axis, at the moment of inertia. Let sheer force = f.**

She then begins to assign values to each variable or term in order to find the maximum bending moment.

$$E\,(fy) = 0$$

A summation of the forces in the Y-direction should be equal to zero

With this place-setting, she can then begin to solve for a numerical value.

---

Your math class is so important because anything you build or engineer needs precision applied mathematics -- calculations that are 100% sound. Inaccurate math causes software systems to collapse, bridges to crumble, tall buildings to crash.

Here is a semi-famous episode in which a small error in calculation led to a gigantic calamity: Lake Peigneur.

Lake Peigneur in central Louisiana was once a small, 10-foot-deep freshwater lake.

On the morning of November 20, 1980, the crew of an oil rig on little Lake Peigneur ran into a small problem.

Their large 14-inch drill bit became stuck as it was digging for oil.

The oil rig crew soon realized that the bit was trapped in crystal salt. They were expecting to hit salt, but not for another hundred feet.

When they attempted to free the drill bit, they heard popping noises. The rig started to tilt. The crew jumped off the rig and headed for the shore. Shortly thereafter, the crew watched as the 150-foot oil rig disappeared into the 10-foot-deep lake.

The lake water was being sucked violently into the empty salt mine below, with catastrophic results. A circular maelstrom of rushing water formed, like a colossal bathtub draining.

Soon the entire contents of the lake -- 13 barges, a fishing boat, some trees, a house, and half of an island -- was consumed in the massive whirlpool. Luckily, no lives were lost.

What happened?

A tiny error in mathematics.

The counting was correct; the assumptions were wrong.

The engineers had known that a salt mine lay beneath Lake Peigneur -- they made a simple mistake in their calculations. The maps of the lake and the map of the salt mine belonged to slightly different map systems – Mercator and UTM. These two types of maps depicted the land and water s in different scales. An engineer mistook transverse Mercator projection coordinates for UTM coordinates. So the map coordinates did not match up. The engineers inadvertently guided their machinery straight into the empty mine shaft tunnel.

Today Lake Peigneur is the deepest lake in Louisiana.

*-- From an account by Thomas Holland, E& S Magazine, Louisiana*

# VOLUME 2
**Red Cross candy-stripers meet the
most powerful tank ever built.**

# *Simone* and the

# MEAN GIRLS

**Clique-driven young nurses become the lone
defenders of an embattled monastery and field
hospital in rural France. The Battle of
Montcornet (May 17, 1940) begins.**

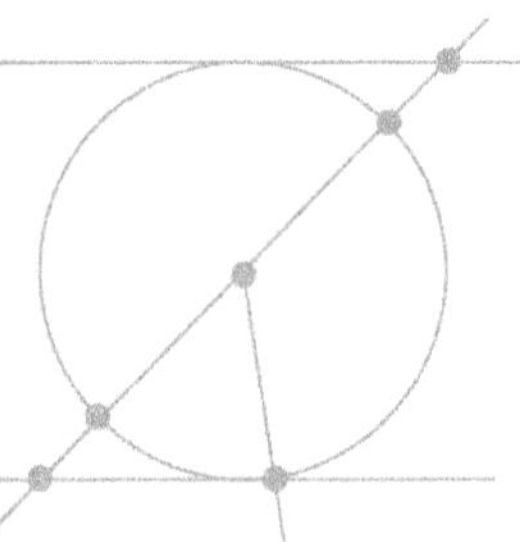

# A PLEASANT MORNING AT
# THE MONASTERY

Mathematics reveals its secrets only to those who
approach it with pure love, for its own beauty.
*-- Archimedes*

"WHAT ARE THESE?" ASKED THE PRETTY GIRL in the candy stripes, Madeline. "These rows of numbers? They're *weird--* "

"Stop it!!" replied the boy in the green-wool uniform. "That's the *signal* notebook -- "

"But the numbers don't make any sense!" pouted Madeline.

"Yes! Maybe that's because they're in code!" The soldier added a brief oath.

"Shouldn't you be on your rounds anyway -- "

The pair had been flirting most of the morning.

"No need," replied pretty Madeline. "Simone is doing quite well on her own."

"Hey Simone!" Madeline called across the infirmary. "Fatso! We have volleyball this afternoon. Remember what happened last time -- "

"Hey, give it a rest," said one of the other boys.

Four schoolgirls, student nurse volunteers, in their candy-stripe uniforms and delicate white hats and clean white aprons, tended the wounded soldiers along the neat rows of cots.

France was at war with Germany.

Her soldiers needed mending.

The lovely, forested grounds of the medieval Cloisters north of the village of Mont-cornet were ideal for recuperation. Pleasant sounds of water running in a brook and birds trilling filled the open first floor of the nunnery.

Simone moved among the patients' beds, offering hope, pouring water, parsing out medications.

"*Et ta gueule,*" replied Simone. "Jump in any time."

"Simone, you can see, even through your eyeglasses," said Charlotte, cruelest of the three. "We're busy conferring with the Security officer s," meaning the boys at the radios.

"Oh! *Graisse cherie!*" Rennie, the small one, chimed in. "You missed a spot! There!"

In the Spring of 1940, France needed all of her resources, all of her people and all of her history, to fend off the overwhelming force of the Third Reich's blitzkrieg. Hitler's Seventh Panzer Division dwarfed all opposition. The Seventh Panzer Division did not distinguish between combatant and schoolchildren, nor did it care to take civilian prisoners.

Suddenly the radio crackled, sharp and loud and grating.

One of the young soldiers pushed Charlotte off his lap as he reached for the radio dials.

The makeshift hospital in the Medieval nunnery also served as one of Montcornet's communications stations.

"*What's that?*" asked Madeline suddenly. "That sound -- "

Everyone stopped to listen to something new.

A deep, guttural, reverberating boom rose, overtaking the radio's thin squawking. It was like thunder rumbling from the basements.

It was a radical, foreign sound, infinitely threatening and sharply out of place in that pastoral, meditative setting.

A machine sound --

Now they heard the snap of crunching branches.

"JESUS!"

Ilyn, the highest-ranking of the teenaged soldiers, pointed down the road which led to the monastery's front drive and portico.

He raised his binoculars.

A monster had suddenly appeared in the road,

It had somehow burst through the hedgerows.

It was now shambling directly towards them no more than a quarter-mile away.

Ilyn cranked the radio generator.

"Hello! Ready One! Ready One! HEY!" he shouted.

"A NAZI TANK just pulled up – "

The creature's rolling treads smashed over the low stone walls that neatly divided the road from the orchards.

"But what are we supposed to do?"

A jarring BOOM! sound --

An explosive concussion blew them out of their seats and sent a shower of stone shards across the infirmary.

"Where did that come from-- "

Bewildered, blinking, the soldiers and nurses sat where they had fallen.

The artillery had struck above them.

Now they heard bursts of rapid machine-gun fire --

Two bodies fell from the second-story balcony onto the lawn in front of the portico.

"NO! No!" screamed Madeline. "CHARLOTTE. Char, Char, nonono --"

Charlotte was not moving. She lay slumped unnaturally against the wall. Deep stains of blood scarred her nurse's uniform. The blow had been terrible and violent --

"HEY! HEY!" Ilyn screamed into the radio microphone. "HELP! HELP US!"

Rennie cowered beneath a doctors' examination table, streaks of blood in her hair --

One of the boys at the radio started crying.

Madeline moaned in fear, clinging to Ilyn's leg.

"*What do you mean?*" screamed the desperate Ilyn into the receiver. A steady stream of chatter poured out of the speaker.

"How would I know what type of tank it is -- "

"*Königstiger*," shouted Simone from across a row of beds that had been knocked over. "It's a *Royal Tiger*. Can't you see -- ?"

She lifted a patient back into one of the cots.

"DUCK!" screamed Ilyn –

*THOOM!*

The bellow of a second artillery round struck the back wall with tremendous '*thunk!*' and detonated on contact.

The stone floors shook with the impact. The system of masonry and archways supporting the Cloisters trembled.

Outside, steel treads on the gravel road signaled that the death machine was rolling inexorably towards them.

At seventy-five tons, the *Konigstiger* was the heaviest tank in all the Third Reich. The Royal Tiger, most destructive tank ever built, led the Panzer corps. Its long-barreled, high velocity KwK 43 88-millimeter cannon could penetrate five inches of armor at a range of two kilometers. It could kill you up close with two 7.92 MG34 machine guns. Driven by a 16-cylinder, 700-horsepower engine, the Royal Tiger could chase down a flock of Jeeps. Its metal skin of green and brown and charcoal gray marked its source, for surely this death-dealer had risen from the caves of the nether-regions, like its beastly brethren, the bloody-jawed Teuton serpent *Jörmungandr*. the undead *draugr*, who single-handedly slew Nerthus and plagued the armies of Nidhogg, and thrice-cursed Grendel, murderous denizen of the mead halls of Heorot.

"HELP US! HELP!" Ilyn repeated into the radio microphone.

The telegraph clacked in response.

The tank shifted gears. Its motors whined and revved, turret adjusting as its guns took fresh aim.

Ilyn stopped to listen to the earphones. He scribbled frantically in his notebook --

Metal cranked. An orange-gold flame flashed --

*BOOM!* Another round struck with a harpie-like shriek and a rain of heavy frag-ments and shrapnel.

"My eardrums!" screamed Rennie. Blood seeped through her fingers as she tried to cover her ears.

Ilyn fell to the floor, cut almost in two, his body blackened –

Madeline redoubled her screaming at the sight of Ilyn's bloody corpse. She slammed into the medicine cupboards in her hysterical effort to get away.

Death stormed the Cloisters.

Simone pushed Ilyn's body off the chair.

She pulled trembling Rennie to her feet.

She leaned over the transmitter and telegraph.

She found Ilyn's notebook and scanned through its pages. She stopped to look hard at one page in particular.

Here is what she saw written there

10  4  24  23  12  10  /  1  2  12  14  10  4  22  17

6  12  22  10  12  24  /  24  12  4  24

"What, Simone?" cried Rennie, buoyed by the sight of her friend taking action. "Can't we go?"

She wrung her hands to try and keep them from shaking so hard.

"What's it say?"

Simone scribbled on a piece of paper.

The furious Konigstiger entered the courtyard with an angry, guttural *Rrrrrrr --*

Simone swept up a MAS-36 carbine that was leaning against the radio desk. She whacked hard and broke the lock on the weapons closet with the rifle butt. She swung the doors open.

"Come on Rennie! Help me carry this -- "

With effort, Simone plucked one of the big rocket launchers from its rack.

The American- made M1A1 shoulder cannon was a metal tube with attachments and dials stuck onto its shaft, five feet long and fifty pounds heavy.

"Here!" Simone grunted and bade her friend carry the back end of the bazooka.

Rennie hesitated.

In the courtyard, the terrible machine sounds came closer.

"*It's just us*," said Simone. "Either we stop this thing, or everybody dies."

Rennie looked hard at her companion.

"All right."

Brave Rennie wiped her nose. She took a breath, to compose herself.

"I understand. Simone. I understand."

The great cannon cranked to turn to follow them.

The next blast buckled the floors and upended furniture, so that the Cloisters seemed like some distorted imitation of its previous state.

Simone scooped up a satchel heavy with the bazooka's ammunition.

The pair began to make their way up the eastern arm of the foyer, an open corridor which flanked the left side of the wide driveway where the German tank advanced.

The path was blocked by great hulks of shattered stone floors.

"Stay low --" urged Simone.

Stumbling over the debris, they almost dropped the rocket launcher.

The ammo rucksack kept falling from Simone's shoulder.

Her hands could not seem to find a grip --

"Jesus, Simmy!" wailed Rennie. "Do we even know to fire this thing?"

The world had gone mad.

The pair of candy-stripers picked and stumbled their way through the corridor of debris.

"It's just us," said Simone. "Either we stop this thing, or everybody dies."

They could hear the French bullets as they pinged harmlessly off the German tank's sloped walls. One of them ricocheted, barely missing Simone's head.

Rennie lagged. Simone pulled Rennie with her.

"Faster!" urged Simone. It sees us -- "

Simone yanked her companion so hard that her cardigan sweater ripped. The candy-striper uniforms were not made for battle and shredded into rags.

Simone removed her eyeglasses. She wiped drops of sweat and blood from her eyes. but it kept coming --

Three times the path was blocked.

Each time, Simone rallied, and found a new way through the rubble. Often they had to climb at almost vertical angles over great stone blocks.

"I can't -- "

Now Rennie was sobbing uncontrollably. The sleeves of her nurse's uniform were soaked in blood.

They slipped twice, three, four times for each single step forward. They used the shattered balustrades for hand-holds.

"Almost there!" promised Simone.

"I can't make it!" cried Rennie –

Simone yanked them over a boulder that had once been a flagstone –

Another detonation blasted. Two stone walls collapsed. Spinning deadly metal shards whizzed through the air around them, only an angry hiss at their passing.

Finally, the two girls reached an intact balustrade well up the corridor, a spot that gave them a view to the *Konigstiger*'s flank --

The tank turret stopped.

Had it seen them?

Simone managed to prop the bazooka on the railing.

They looked back to see a wounded Madeline waving the giant Red Cross banner and calling to the *Konigstiger*. No one could miss it. Madeline threw a tantrum, screaming rudely at the tank, demanding its attention.

The turret paused.

The turret cranked and turned towards the waving banner –

"Get out!" cried Rennie. "Madeline get out! *It sees you --* "

The Royal Tiger let go a burst of cannon fire.

The stone porch exploded. The banner clattered to the ground, waving pitifully just for a moment as it fell. No more could be heard of Madeline and her tantrum.

The tank's turret gun turned toward the two candy-stripers with the bazooka.

"Jesus! Fire it, Simone!!" screamed Rennie --

The tank had completed its rotation. *Target acquired.*

Simone fired.

*Click*

Now the machine gunner was finding his range --

*Click*

She removed the safety. A deadly hissing shower of cartridges sinking into plaster came closer --

*Click*

She plucked the rocket out of the tube and re-fit it more properly in the bazooka tube –

*Click ---*

The tank's cannon fired. The projectile seemed to jam in its craw.

*Click*

"*Au diable!!*" screamed Simone

*BAM!!*

A *whoosh* like a comet dying and a blur of blue flame --

Red fire --

A sharp pain stabbed Simone's shoulder.

She felt cold acid on her cheek --

The world went black. Wind and heat whirled.

As she was falling, Simone heard the echo of Rennie's calls --

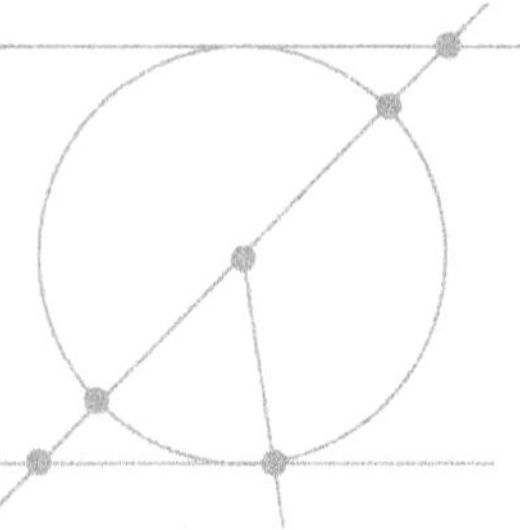

# THE INFIRMARY WARD

It's not a miracle. We just decided to go.
*-- William Broyles Jr.*

THE EYES WERE DEEP BROWN.

Surrounded by dark curls.

The brows slowly came into focus.

It was a young face, a young man's face. Simone could see crinkles at the edge of the eyes. She saw a toughness in the set of the mouth, humor and understanding in the eyes.

These were eyes that had seen many things.

"Ah," came the voice, deep and a little tired.

But it was a kind voice, the voice of a man who listened.

She looked up from the hospital bed.

"Am I dead?" asked Simone.

"No," the man replied. "Not today."

The soldier was young, maybe 20. The patch on his shoulder identified him as an officer in the Fourth Armored Division, France's premier tank battalion.

He propped up her pillow. She winced. She thanked him. He poured a glass of water for her.

"That shoulder rocket," said the young officer. "The M1-A1. Some of our best men can't lift and fire it properly."

"I didn't have much choice," Simone replied.

She looked around. The infirmary, the main room on the back or west-facing flank of the Cloisters complex, was busy with mid-morning activities.

With his help, she took a long drink of water.

"You got way too close. But you knew that."

"Didn't want to miss," explained Simone.

Simone tried and failed to sit up straight.

She closed her eyes, as if imagining what she wanted to do. She took a deep breath.

"That tank commander trained under the *Hauptsturmfuhrer*,"the young officer told her. "Wittman. He was one of their rising stars."

She tried again.

She managed to sit all the way up. She flexed the fingers of her left hand.

"I don't know who Wittman is, but that *salaud* was going to kill practically every-one I know-- "

She faltered, falling sideways.

"Whoa, stallion," he said encouragingly. "Easy."

A trio of soldiers walked up to her bedside. They saluted Simone. They murmured, praising her bravery, and her aim. One handed her a brownie.

"Okay boys," said the young officer at her side. "That's great. Now clear out, give her some room -- "

"What happened?" Simone asked.

"Your round ignited the tank's ammo. Blasted the turret eighty feet into the air. Five crewmen died. We captured the sixth. Man, is he unhappy ..."

She shook her head, as if to clear her memory.

He took out a cigarette

A passing nurse struck it out of his mouth.

He mumbled a protest and picked it up from the floor.

"My arm really hurts," said Simone.

"The recoil," he explained. "Almost broke your arm."

They sat together for a minute, not speaking. Simone's mind was clearing.

"How did you break that code so fast?" he asked her.

She removed a piece of paper from the apron of the uniform draped over the chair. She took the paper and carefully spread it, smoothing it as she did.

This was the code she had taken from Ilyn's notebook, and below the numbers, its translation:

$$10 \ 4 \ 24 \ 23 \ 12 \ 10 \ / \ 1 \ 2 \ 12 \ 14 \ 10 \ 4 \ 22 \ 17$$

$$6 \ 12 \ 22 \ 10 \ 12 \ 24 \ / \ 24 \ 12 \ 4 \ 24$$

TARGET fuel tank center rear

"Just like that?"

"I could see it," Simone shrugged. "We practiced the tables at school."

"You and Gauss," he joked. She laughed at the reference.

"I'm in my first year at Aix-Marseille," he said.

They heard a commotion and turned to see --

"Simmy!" came a familiar voice.

"Simmy, you did it!"

It was Rennie. Two of her teeth were missing, and she walked with a limp, yet she hugged her friend with genuine joy and called her 'Sweetheart.'

"You were so brave! I was such a coward --"

"You were heroic, *cherie* -- " said Simone.

"I'm so sorry we said such mean things to you. I don't know what we were thinking.

"And now -- Madeline and Char are - they're both -- "

Rennie began crying.

"I keep seeing them. When I close my eyes -- all that blood -- "

"Okay, okay, just great, thank you -- " The young officer signaled one of his men to escort Rennie back to her bed.

An inspector from d'Arc-en-Barroios had arrived. She had brought orderlies and medical students and American medicines, component s of a full apothecary, with her. She was now busily overseeing an expansion of the nunnery's medical operations.

A small surgery had been constructed in one corner, and two triage rooms. White vats of antiseptic were being stacked under rows of newly installed wash basins. Now Simone could see medical students in white coats and plumbers and toolboxes and pipes and joints and anesthesia tubing scattered about. Along the south portico, horses and carriages being prepped for service as an ambulance corps. There seemed to be an urgency to the preparations. Armed combat loomed. All of the field‑ hospital services would be needed soon.

"What did that girl mean, 'all the things we said'?" asked the young officer.

Simone shrugged.

"Huh! She owes you her life. *Sa mère.* So do I. So does every man and woman in this castle."

A senior nurse with warm hands checked Simone's temperature. Murmuring, she dwelt on Simone, tucking her in and fussing with her hair and calling her 'the heroine of Montcarnet.'

"We're planning to pay the Bosch a little visit," said the young officer casually, when they were alone.

To their left, among the rows of cots, an altercation over morphine broke out between a supervisor and a rowdy patient.

"Maybe you'd like to come along … "

For the first time, Simone, schoolgirl‑turned‑ soldier, warrior‑nurse, child of Mont‑cornet, turned to look directly at her companion.

A scar along the young officer's boyish nose became visible when he smiled.

He raised an eyebrow, just slightly, as if to repeat the question.

"Yes," replied Simone.

She had seen up close one of the shambolic, evil‑brewed demons that now stalked the innocent lands of Gaul.

She preferred not to wait for the next one to show up in her home village, but to go and find it, meet it, armed, and destroy it in its lair. If she could.

"Yes, I will go."

# TOM'S NOTES

For all their sophistication (Maybach engines, 88 mm guns, heavier armor, wider tracks), the German tanks were less dependable, especially later in the war. Rushed production did not help. Worker sabotage played a part, as well. In Cornelius Ryan's "The Last Battle," the author references Jean Boutin, a 20-year-old machinist from Paris labored in German armaments plant. "Boutin and some Dutch workers had been sabotaging tank parts for years."

The Russian T-34 tank was far less sophisticated than the German Tiger, but more reliable. Seventy per cent of its parts were interchangeable.

The math used for secret codes is window-dressing math. Other stories – the Chinese story, the Mogollons story, for sure – have stronger and deeper math content, math that is more central to the story, but I felt that needed a straightforward, high-velocity story at or near the beginning of the collection.

Carl Gauss is mentioned in both the tank story and the first Rupa story.

Carl Gauss was a child math prodigy in 18th century Braunschweig, or Brunswick, now part of Lower Saxony, Germany.

A famous story (possibly true) has Carl, at age seven, attending primary school. The story goes that his lazy Instructor, hoping to keep his classroom busy while he took a coffee break, assigned them the following:

"Add all the numbers between 1 and 100 and give me the sum."

The Instructor assumed it would take some time, and turned to go.

But young Gauss amazed him by piping up almost immediately:

"5050, sir."

To Gauss, the problem was structural, and the answer was easy to see. He had simply added the numbers in pairs - the first and the last, the second and the second to last and so on, observing that 1+100=101, 2+99=101, 3+98=101 ... so the total would be 50 lots of 101, which is 5050.

Here is how the formula looks:

## Find the sum of the consecutive numbers 1-100:

$$(100 / 2)(1 + 100)$$

$$50(101) = 5,050$$

Carl Gauss went on to become a major figure in mathematics history.

# VOLUME 3
### Geometry for a queen.

# Isoke and the ARCHITECT

Young Isoke and her brothers attend the Igue festival, intent on buying a bull calf for their village. They bravely thwart an assassination attempt on Queen Nala. The Queen makes Isoke a gift of books, and the consequences change Benin history.

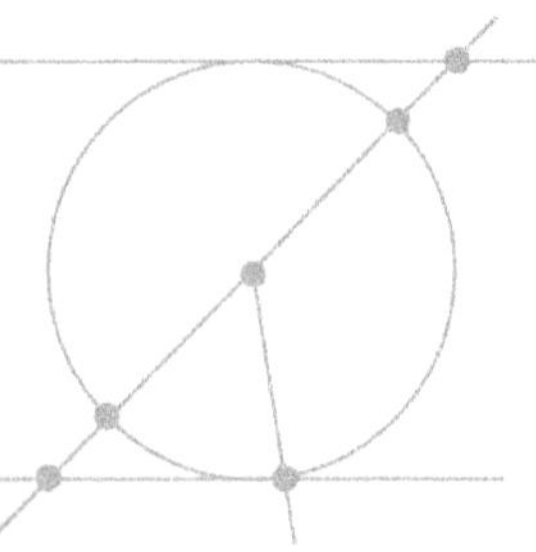

# ISOKE AND THE SLAYERS

In African history, we have evidence of counting
and numeration systems, games and puzzles,
geometry, graphs, record-keeping, money,
weights, and measures, etc.
-- *Paulus Gerdes, A History of Mathematics In Africa*

"COME!" URGED ISOKE. "WE CAN'T BE LATE!"
The first day of the Igue festival was in full swing.

With a grunt, the girl shouldered one of the ropes.

"The Mundari are thoughtless merchants. They'll let their best calves go first-- "

She pulled the big-wheeled cart through the festival grounds.

Six of her brothers pulled alongside her.

"You're a long way from home, *umngeele*," called a smiling Xhosa woman standing
before a tiger- patterned curtain. She used a term that meant something between
"borderlander" and "boon-docker." She waved invitingly.

"Save some time for me on the way back," Simtho told her. She laughed. The other
brothers, even grim-faced Ypiku, enjoyed this exchange.

The little outlander family, led by the skinny girl Isoke, made their way past the
vendors' stands and the livestock pens and the tapestry displays.

Isoke had visited the grounds the night before, to map out their route.

The festival grounds were a celebration of symbols and numbers – different tribes'
runes and patterns spoke of beliefs, cosmology, rituals, totem birds and animals. Seers

threw sign-marked rune-stones and announced destinies. Hooded hawks perched on their masters' arms. Teams of boys jousted, their patterned vests identifying each clan. A tethered panther paced to and fro in a large cage, its eyes resting on passers-by.

The fair seemed boundless. They could only see parts of the whole.

"Stay strong, brothers!"urged the girl. "We are almost there -- "

Only fourteen years old, Isoke was the matriarch of her clan and the acting chieftain of the Atakora, a small, once- undisciplined tribe of hunters in the remote Cotinou region, on the eastern peripheries of the kingdoms of Benin.

They wore their bows and shields on their backs, for all outlanders are hunters, and all hunters care to keep their weapons close by.

"Here we go – this way -- "

Isoke had been saving for over a year to buy a bull-calf, to sire the village's heifers. A healthy herd would change the fortunes of her people, that much she knew. She was determined to do right. Her ingenious new design for the baskets was water-tight and had become much-favored among the river tribes. As word spread and others came to see, and acquire, the baskets, she had been able to collect two bags full of sarafu, the coins forged by the brass workers of Igbo Ukwu, coins which the traders of the steppes used as currency. These she would use to buy a fine bull-calf.

The Mundari bred a handsome line of cattle.

"*There!*" called Isoke. "The Mundari pennants are just beyond -- "

They rounded a corner.

They had come to a sort of open space, or plaza.

It was the royal court.

They saw Nala, Queen of the Benin lands, the festival's hostess, as she sat presiding over dances and livestock displays and various goings-on.

Beside her stood the wiry Portuguese, her most trusted advisor.

Behind Nala's throne stood the royal guard, fine strong warriors in their war paint and feathered head-gear and imposing shields.

Around the perimeters of the plaza were arranged the Queen's closest allies, some of the most powerful tribes of the Benin nation.

Isoke suddenly stopped.

*Something is wrong…*

"Why are we stopping?" asked Osahar angrily.

Isoke crouched and held her left hand high.

She fisted the hand.

Now a second time. …

Simtho, who was closest to Isoke in age and temperament, saw that his sister's shoulders were tensed, trembling slightly.

"*Something is very, very wrong,*" murmured the girl.

With a signal, she bade her brothers notch their bows.

They did so on the instant, not asking why.

On their left, at the head of the plaza, was the royal court –

On their right, among the assembled wagons, stood a broad-berthed cart. Its open bay concealed behind a tapestry of moons and stars.

Without warning a blood-curdling scream tore from behind the curtain.

The tapestry was ripped away --

A clutch of roaring painted warriors appeared in its place.

The assassins burst out, spears raised, '*DEATH TO NALA!!*' on their lips --

Isoke ran straight at them --

"Wait! Wait!" cried Ypiku, the eldest of her brothers, the cautious, rule-abiding first born --

But there was no waiting.

There never is. In a real life, the most fateful events can unfold at the snap of a finger –

The ragged-toothed assassins were young and big-shouldered, fearful killers bristling with knives. One wielded a short-sword, of the European fashion.

They wore leopard skins.

Isoke grabbed a torch from the Xhosa and hurled it crossways, to trip the slayers as they advanced.

Three of them toppled.

A round of her brothers' arrows struck down the front-line assassins before they had closed half the distance across the plaza –

A slayer hurled a spear directly at Queen Nala --

Nala, a tall, fierce woman, plucked the spear from its trajectory mid-air and returned it with force.

It impaled the slayer with a 'Thunk!'--

Now the Portagee swept a pair of pistols from his waistband, aimed and fired with loud double '*Booms!* --

Two slayers descended on Isoke, who had drawn a blade of her own --

Osahar appeared. He stood in front of his sister, shielding her –

Osahar kicked one slayer's legs out from under him and garroted the second with his bow-string, until the bow snapped --

The royal guard, unused to actual fighting, fled --

The Queen threw herself into the shield-splintering melee.

The Portagee's sword flashed cleverly.

Half-mad with frenzy, brave Simtho leapt on the back of a slayer, only to earn a deep wound in the shoulder for the effort --

But the leopard skins had planned poorly, for now – now that their initial rush had been blunted – they were trapped.

Now a dash of hunters from the Yoruba and Xhosa and (surprisingly!) Swahili delegations ran to the aid of their Queen --

For a long moment all was confusion and blood-lust. Terrible cries and shouts of Surrender! rose. The pretend-warriors who brag of their deeds but care not to wield a sword when blood is spilled huddled behind the throne.

It ended in a moment, as it had started.

And when the deadly combat had stilled, and when the dust and smoke had settled, it was the scrawny border girl, Isoke, who stood in the center of the plaza, still and tall among the fallen.

Shivering hilts and bloody spears and moaning bodies surrounded her.

In the distance, drums started up.

Isoke surveyed the square.

Now a war chant rose, in celebration of Queen Nala's great victory, and the selfless bravery of her subjects.

The Portagee raised his sword in salute.

He shook his weapon.

"How did you know?" he called to Isoke. "What gave them away?"

She wiped her blade on the fabric of her skirt.

"Geometry," the border girl replied.

"How did you know?" he called. She wiped her blade on the fabric of her skirt. "Geometry," the border girl replied.

*Wikimedia Commons*

# AN AUDIENCE WITH THE QUEEN

Geometry is still there when the rest of our
reasoning mind is stripped away.
*-- Jordan Ellenberg*

"WHAT IS 'GEOMETRY'?" ASKED QUEEN NALA.
They had settled in the safe confines of her royal tent.

"'*Maumbo ya nambari*,'" Isoke replied. "Numbers and shapes."

"I was here last night," she said. "Those are not the Fulbe colors," she explained, naming the mesa tribe from whose ranks the marauders had come. "Only the Zulu use that pattern, and only when they are going to battle.

"The positioning was all wrong. You could see that all the networks had been broken.

"I knew something bad was behind that curtain -- "

"You are the basket-weavers. Border folk," asserted the Queen. "From across the veldt."

"Aye," replied Isoke.

"You must have met the French Navigator, when he was alive," stated the Portagee pointedly, as he reloaded his pistols.

"Aye," replied Isoke again, somewhat surprised. "When I was a child."

The white man nodded, as if this explained much.

"I know Arabic," Isoke added, a simple-seeming statement which meant far more than it appeared to mean. "I can read and write."

"Just so," countered the white man. "And you must be the one who built that bridge across the Lesotho."

"Yes," answered Isoke. "The cursed planks would not behave. It took two weeks."

She took a fig from the platter which Osahar offered in her direction.

"Enough of your imbecilic questions, English," interrupted Queen Nala.

"Not too imbecilic, Mistress of Earth and Sky," intoned the Portagee. "These are points on a line." The Portagee tucked the pistols back into the cumberbund at his waist. "Points on a line …"

"Whatever that means," commented the Queen, irritated.

Nala, Savage Queen of all Benin, had not risen to power in the bloody tribal wars of Benin by contemplating mysteries. She stood and circled to address the border girl directly, a spear in one hand and a flagon in the other.

"Now!" The Queen stamped her spear on the dirt floor.

"Tell me of these geometries, my girl."

"Are they useful in war? Do they predict the future? Can they thwart my enemies? My empire expands. Certain regions resist. As you see. The Igala send assassins to kill me -- "

Brother Ypiku returned to the tent from retrieving their arrowheads.

"A proper understanding of ratios and integers can enhance any activity, I'm sure," replied Isoke. "I am but a beginner -- "

"Hah! You said 'enhance'!" chortled Nala. "You meant to say enrich-- "

"No," replied Isoke. "No, geometry has nothing to do with wealth, Majesty."

Simtho and the other brothers listened carefully to this exchange, looking up between bites of fruit.

Nala considered this statement.

She ate three coated yam-sections and a handful of peanuts.

"You have unusual features, border girl" she said to Isoke. "You will be a most alluring woman. Soon enough." She used a term, *umtsalane*, that carried an extra meaning, something beyond beauty.

"Your highness," said Isoke.

Isoke stood to her full height.

"You seem like a nice lady. I'm glad we could help.

"We have to go now.

"Best to leave the village of Idiwekazi and the Atakora folk out of all your royal deliberations. Plans of empire. Kingdoms. Any such. We seek only to be left alone."

Nala snorted at this. The Portagee bade Nala restrain herself.

"Only this," said he to Isoke. "You must allow the Queen to bestow a gift. She is the fairest of rulers. Both wise and just. Most generous."

Isoke hesitated.

"We came to Igue to buy a bull calf, Great One," she said to Nala. "A second such beast would surely be a boon -- "

"It is done!" exclaimed Nala. "We grant a *second* and a *third* bull calf to the brave Atakora!" ordered the monarch. "*Ayeeee!*"

Her entourage of cowards joined in.

"They risked their lives and thwarted a most despicable attempt on the royal body," the Queen announced, arms raised. "Nala is red death to her foes. Golden light to her loyal friends. Ayeeee!"

The Queen nodded to Isoke and her brothers, a signal for the supplicants to bend the knee.

The border girl and her brothers turned and took their leave without ceremony. Simtho smiled and waved as they departed, not wanting to be rude.

> **Best to leave the village of Idiwekazi out of all your royal deliberations. Plans of empire. Kingdoms. Any such.**

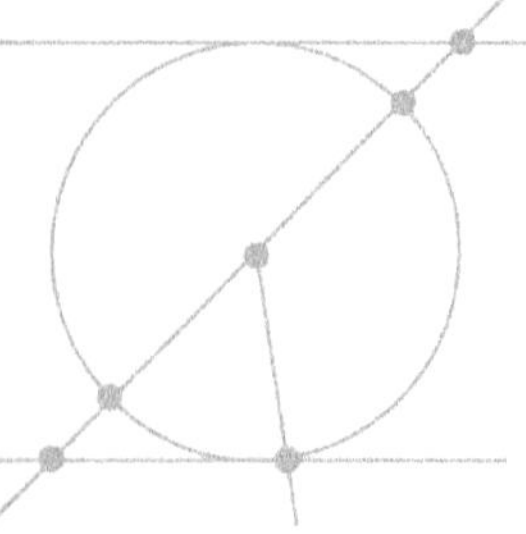

# IDIWEKAZI



A YEAR AND TWO MONTHS AFTER THAT fateful morning at the Igue festival, a two-story wooden structure loomed over the meadow and the little pond at the edge of the village of Idiwekazi, home of the Atakora, in the region of Cotilou.

"Pull!" called Isoke.

The assembled crew of twenty villagers pulled on the ropes.

The heavy beam slowly rose from the ground and swung into place.

The tall cranes creaked.

The load hovered slightly.

"Here it comes" cried Simtho.

"Have the bevel joints ready! Joists! Ready! Ho!" called Isoke.

She had it all in her mind. Sometimes, she would close her eyes and walk it through, step by step.

She felt sure that a sturdy two-story wooden shelter for the livestock could be built.

It was a barn she was imagining, and after that a farm, and after that a small city.

The first key was how to build high. How to use shapes in order to build high, and build big.

The visions were explicit and clear. Yet they came in fits and starts. She could not see all of it.

A three-story wooden crane loomed, rickety and ambitious, above the scaffolding. Taut ropes and braided vines holding the beam hung from the crane.

Boys on tall ladders help guide the beam down through the scaffolding and into place. It was the centerpiece of the new structure.

The build was surrounded by haystacks.

The three bull-calves, the heifers, and several progeny watched the goings-on with mild interest from behind fences constructed in a cross=hatch design.

"Hold the roof – hey!"

A sudden gust of wind from the valley floor caught the beam's broad side.

A boy lunged, trying to correct the rope's trajectory –

It swung too wide, out side the framework. Cords of bundled vine and ropes snapped, unused to such a heavy weight in a position this lateral --

One cord went slack. A villager's neck was caught when it was pulled tight – she went sailing upwards --

The crane's neck snapped --

The load crashed through the woven palm-frond roof --

Section by section, the scaffolded house collapsed, walls falling in with exhausted sighs. The entire structure lay in a dusty heap.

Boys leapt free to land safe and laughing in the haystacks. Ladders toppled.

The throat-caught villager was cut down.

"That's precision work," commented Osahara, using Isoke's own phrase against her.

She moved to kick him. He dodged, jeering. She tossed a plank after him and swore, but in good cheer, for she well remembered that sour-faced Osahara had been first to leap between her and death that day at Igue.

"It seems almost right," said Simtho encouragingly.

"It's doomed," she declared, using a long, low curse. "I did everything wrong."

"You'll figure it out."

"I'm missing something. Something important." Her voice was beyond disgusted. "I'm a failure. A fraud. It's all a waste, Simmus …"

"Let's see what the cooks have for dinner," suggested Simtho.

"May be that venison stew that you like."

"I told you about this," said the girl Isoke solemnly to Queen Nala. Her voice was cold and hard.

The two stood facing one another on the high road, on the bluffs which protected the northern approach to the nestled village of Idiwekazi.

Nala, on horseback, loosed the reins, so her steed could graze while his mistress parlayed.

"Yes, you did."

Behind the mounted Queen of the Benin Kingdoms, Mistress of Land and Sky, trailed a caravan of troops, wagons, and livestock, stretching down the foothills which protected the village of Idiwekaze, home to the little border tribe of the Atakora, with its remarkable young matriarch. Cavalry and archers, spear-wielders and rows of infantry awaited the con-versation, banners waving.

In the distance, a flock of water-birds – terns – paused in their migration to execute a swirl, a murmuration, in which the aggregate moved in a complex, coordinated pattern in. No member of the swarm struck another. Neighboring birds moved together yet apart, aligning their speed and direction, exchanging positions so those inside the funnel traded places with those on the peripheries. The terns funneled in unison into a down-ward switchback called kurudi nyuma. Its appearance was a powerful omen, although neither of the women took note.

The girl, almost two years older than she had been that day at Igue, stood with her arms crossed.

She blocked the road to the village of Idiwekazi. Her brothers stood in a cluster behind her.

A breeze from the east ruffled the feathers in her hair.

Nala dismounted. She shooed away her attendants, except for one.

"I was right," she said as she neared Isoke. "You have grown. Hewu! You have a look."

Nala took two cloth satchels from the attendant and tossed them on the ground in front of the border girl.

"What is this?" asked Isoke.

"A gift. The Portagee said you would like it."

Isoke bent to lift one of the satchels. It was heavy.

"And where is he?"

"Somewhere in the North, no doubt," she continued, 'the North' meaning Europe, England, Scandinavia, Ireland, Iceland and Greenland, the various states of Germany, Eastern Russia or possibly arctic parts of the New World.

Isoke opened one of the satchels.

She pulled out a journal. In her hands, the leather cover seemed aged and streaked, yet its pages of neatly ledgered handwriting were crisp and dry --

"Geometries, umngelee," said Nala. "Numbers and shapes and words."

Nala's men dropped more such satchels.

"Books and books filled with them. Accounts of rain and sun, plants to eat, trade routes, migrations. Many numbers. Many words. Much language." She named the African Navigator, whose records these were.

"Such things in which you delight."

Now there lay six satchels in all.

# Accounts of rain and sun, plants to eat, trade routes, migrations. Many numbers. Many words. Much language. Such things in which you delight.

"The Portagee said that I should tell you that you owe me nothing for this," said Nala. "These are freely given."

She gestured in a royal manner.

Isoke bent to leaf through the books and journals and maps.

She found works by the Arab mathematician Thabit Ibn Qurra, including his sundials. Also there were tomes detailing the cubes and algebra of Al-Mahan, and illustrated books of Corinthian engineers. Here was Herodotus, and papyri stamped with the mark of the Alexandria Library. She glanced through what appeared to be a copy of a copy of Leonardo's journal, and histories, too, Greek and Sumerian, and one small volume on canals and water-management that appeared to be in Chinese.

Above, the flock of terns wheeled upward, then swirled and set out to exit Africa, angled sharply upward. They turned towards the green fields of France, whence they were bound.

"Queen Nala," said Isoke at length. "These are gifts, gifts which ... these ... these ... these books ... and the knowledge they contain. They augur great things for my people. They are useful beyond measure."

"Ah! Yes yes. You are honest, girl-of-the-numbers. You are pleased. It is well. He said you would like them."

"How did the Portagee come into their possession?"

"Among the English. Who can say?"

"How can I repay you, Majesty?"

"Only if you insist," said the Queen.

"I do," said Isoke.

"Then we ask only a small favor in return," replied Queen Nala.

"I need a battle plan to crush the rebels who conspire against me.

"Designs for war. Magical weapons too, if you can," she added. "The Zulu are brash."

Nala looked out over the steppes, then at the foothills of Cotinou. The terns, in the distance, seemed to pause, so as to hear her.

"The waters are rising, Geometry Girl. The veldt tribes do not care to pay my tributes. Yet they call for my armies at the first blush of Arab bandits.

"Now the Fulbe and three of the delta tribes ally with them."

The Queen snapped her fingers.

The attendant, a stout young woman with markings of the Yoruba in her hair and on her clothing, stepped forward.

"This is my new counsel. Her name is Esigie."

Esigie bowed low.

"She is not smart," the Queen explained, "but she is most loyal."

"Wise One," said the Yoruba girl to Isoke.

"You needn't bow to me," said Isoke, bending down to help Esigie up. "Call me by my name. 'Isoke.' I bear no titles."

"She gives you maps and charts of the Osemwade fields," explained Nala, "as well as our reports on the rebel forces. We plan to meet them there, in battle, early next year.

"Now we take our leave, to council with the Murabaraba. The Swahili, also in attendance. Ye Gods.

"We return in two moons. In the hopes you will help good Queen Nala, humble Nala, that she may crush Benin's foes. And protect her loyal subjects."

Satisfied with that pronouncement, Queen Nala clicked her fingers while moving her arms in a grand circle about her whole being, as if drawing a sort of wrap or screen around herself. She repeated the movement. The crisp sounds of her fingers snapping rang in the morning air.

She and all her escort took leave, headed south and east.

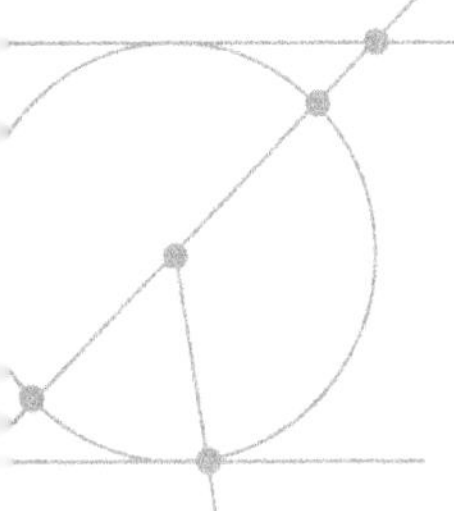

# NALA SEES

<hr>

During the seventeenth century, the
military and administrative chiefs came to
overshadow the king,
-- *Osarhieme Benson Osadolor, M.,*
*The Military System of Benin Kingdom*

<hr>

ISOKE HAD THE ONE INSIGHT, YET IT was far-reaching: that everything we can see and touch is composed of smaller elements, and that these various-appearing constructive or universal elements were themselves somehow related.

It had been confirmed to her at age five, when she stood with her father atop Mount Sokbaro, looking down at the river valley, holding a leaf in her hand. The pattern of the river tributaries on the valley floor and the pattern of the leaf veins were one and the same.

Among the many and wildly varied, dissimilar shapes of things, she knew, there was a commonality. If she could but understand these fundamental shapes, she could help her people. She would be able to build things. The Lesotho bridge was an early experiment. She and her brothers had gone back to restore and rebuild it six times.

<hr>

"There."

Isoke swore bitterly.

"No, that's wrong! Simtho, keep the – here! *Damn!* Give it to me -- "

"Don't tell me what to do!" rejoined Simtho.

"The cloth must stay beneath it," insisted the girl. "You clod. There! Now. Just ... so -- "

Carefully, Isoke lowered the heavy stone slab so that it rested upon the eggshell. "You'll break it," Simtho warned.

She had carefully shaved the shell of an ostrich egg and placed it on a cloth, on a tall tabletop hewed from a tree stump.

The half-shell, smooth-edged, seemed capable of bearing any weight.

The stone which Isoke lowered on top of it should have crushed it.

She released her fingers.

The fragile-looking shell held strong.

"Isoke," muttered Simtho hopefully as the pair stared at the spectacle. "Izzy-okaye. Izzimawami ... "

The empty eggshell, so small and fragile, should not have been able to bear that weight ...

"Is it magic?" sked Simtho.

He clapped his hands loudly, as if to wake the egg up to what was happening.

"No," proclaimed Isoke. "It holds steady because of its shape. It is a perfect shape.

"See how the arch of the shell s distributes the weight. The downward force. It is perfectly even, so that no one part of the shell buckles."

They walked around the table.

The egg remained unbothered. Blithe.

Isoke sketched how she imagined the weight was being shared, and in what sequence she would need to add weight to an archway based on that same principal.

Once she understood the mathematics, she could use arches to construct a sturdy barn, and a house two stories tall, and the storage bins she dreamed of.

Already, wooden models of the aqueduct archway she had seen in one of the books' pictures were being raised on stone pedestals.

Simtho added a second slab on top of the eggshell.

Now fifty *debens* of rock sat suspended there, leaning fully on the little egg-dome.

Still it held.

"This is magic, surely, Sim," intoned Isoke. "Sim. Simotho. Sim *salabim*."

A water tower could be next.

"I think we're getting somewhere," concluded Isoke.

Simtho nodded.

Isoke walked to the table to consult the picture in the book again.

She placed her hand on the picture.

The image had haunted her for weeks, ever since she had first seen it.

It was a picture of a storm drain.

A grated street drain, as you see in any European city. So that when the rains fill the streets with water, the runoff has somewhere to go.

It was not the image of the drain itself which haunted her, but its many implications: it clearly meant that there existed an entire system beneath the city.

"Is the city built on platforms?" she asked Simtho. "What is down there? Is it above them, as well?"

Simtho did not know.

She had heard of palaces built within caves, one in China, in the northeast provinces, where librarians guarded tomes and scrolls and maps from the early hours of mankind, where open bowls of rice absorbed moisture, so as to better protect the papyrus from weather, and the passage of time. Is this city like that? Built within a larger structure?

*What else is down there?*

She regarded her own village, with its modest huts and dirt floors and wandering chickens.

*How do they do that?*

"Why are we building all these new things?" asked Osahar one night as they all ate dinner around the big fires.

*"What's the point?"*

Before loyal Simtho could leap across the open benches and strangle his brother, Ypiku spoke up.

"Shouldn't we just hunt and fish, like the other tribes?" asked the eldest of the brothers.

"All this 'geometry.' It's strange," said Osahar, using a low Urdu term which was also used to suggest 'European' or 'from a foreign land,' the subtext being mostly negative.

The deep, still silence which followed this remark indicated that Osahar was not alone in wondering.

"Why are we trying so hard to be different?" asked Ypiku.

"We are happy. As we always were."

"You are both morons, that is what!" said Simtho, mightily displeased.

"But we are happy morons," replied Osahar. "We know nothing of 'try-bangles' and 'multiplikers.' Yet our people have managed, over these many generations..."

Isoke nodded thoughtfully and finished eating the roasted meat and herb-cooked vegetables (from her gardens) on her plate. She soaked up the last gravy on the plate with a piece of bread she had baked.

"Well," she said.

"Ypiku, you are my eldest brother.

"Osahar, you saved my life at the fairgrounds. And several times before then.

"I cannot cross you. I do not choose to cross any of you," she added. "You're my family."

*Uh-oh*, the expressions on the faces around the campfire seemed to say.

"So, no," concluded Isoke. "We don't have to do ... all of this."

The others waited for her to say more.

Isoke plucked a pomegranate from among the fruits and took a bite. She eyed the setting sun, and gave no indication of further comment.

This meant one of two things.

First, that she would secede from the Atakora and form her own tribe, bringing all the women with her. Or, second, that she would join the neighboring Fon, whose chieftain, Oyegun, had twice offered to marry her.

New, profound misgivings floated in the dusky air, joining the smoke and the darkening light of the fine evening.

"Let's vote!" urged Simtho.

Young Simtho understood the stakes, now.

He made eye contact with each of his brothers, and cousins, and tribal members of all ages, so that the way of things was unmistaken: *Now or Never.*

Challenge Isoke now, or accept her, Geometry and all.

"A show of hands, brothers!" called Simtho.

The group considered. No one moved.

Perhaps the members of the Idiwekazi were remembering the ease at which the Isoke-built catapults had demolished wooden targets half a league distant, or the value of the Isoke-designed paddocks and barns for their cattle, or the small wonders of her irrigated gardens. They had come into being just as she imagined.

"*Points on a line,*" remarked Ypiku inscrutably.

He repeated the phrase, not knowing what it meant but suspecting it might be germane (if neutral).

Then a fit of coughing seized Osahar, followed by extensive advice from a young shaman, who called on specific ancestors to aid good Osahar, then a protracted round of back-pounding and drinking water, and more coughing. The young shaman himself left to fetch a remedy.

Dinner was over.

Isoke's leadership was not brought up again.

In the silver-blue moonlight, Queen Nala caught her breath.

"*Am I dreaming?*" Nala whispered to Esiglie.

"I see it too, my liege," came the reply.

The two women had crawled half a league, up the slope of the high burm which overlooked the village of Idiwekaze ... or what had once been that hamlet.

In place of huts and fire pits were two- and three-storied scaffolded structures, support arches placed all along the bases. A stream burbled along the village margin, tucked in a bed of set stones. She could see a great wheel half-built that moved with the passing water, and a hut of smoothed surfaces next to it.

Below stood half a dozen scattered watch-towers, and cranes, and a longhouse, and half a barn. Cattle dozed safe behind wood fences, patterned in the same manner as the thatched roofs.

Even more incredible was the slope of terraced fields rising into the distance beyond the village. Moonlight shone clear along the irrigation canals which fed the gardens. It seemed to the midnight observers that all manner of produce sprouted along those rows.

*What sorcery is this?*

As her eyes adjusted to the moonlight, Nala could make out a pathway from the village downhill to a large wharf by the river. She squinted and made out the contours of a boathouse, and boats of exotic design resting in their berths.

This was sorcery beyond all comprehension.

Nala did not understand these structures, not in their particulars, nor could she ken the philosophy which gave them rise. But she knew what she was seeing: it was the beginnings of an empire. This was a phenomenon whole in itself, a vision, a system, a thing with great purpose, designed and built with a sure hand and utter command. Whoever built this could also build a span of rule over Benin as mighty as those Stygian empires, those fearsome kingdoms of Hammurabi and Set and Atlantis, lost in the mists of time.

Nala stepped away, deeply shaken. What she had seen called into question her entire belief system.

That night, speaking to Esigie, Nala first used the term that would follow the Idi-wekazi girl for the rest of her days (though that interval was not to be so very long).

It was the only title that Isoke herself would eventually allow to be spoken in her presence.

*Mbunifu..*

The Architect.

The next morning, they met by the river, half a league south of Idiwekazi.

Little was said of the council, other than that the talks dragged on and that, at some point, HoHoe of the Narinta had needed to have his throat slit.

Great was the surprise among Nala's men when Osahar and the young hunters of the Atakora wheeled out three small swivel cannons, long buried in mud, exposed when the riverbed had been diverted. The cannons were made of brass, similar to those first introduced along the coastal forts by Vaz Coelho (although they could not know that).

Next came flat wagons bearing thirty crossbows of hard wood, iroko and mahogany and a new design, for the books had shown Isoke how to bend wood with steam. The weapons had a quick release and easy reloading, advanced over any that had been seen in those lands. Demonstrations left the Benin commanders impressed with the weapons' accuracy.

Nala herself seemed most delighted when she was presented with four low-slung catapults of uncanny range. The brothers showed the Benin commanders the apparatus' designs and destructive powers and gave them schematic drawings, instructions as to how to manufacture more.

The biggest reception came when Osahara tossed two thunder gourds, crude incendiary weapons which you may know as Greek fire. They exploded, louder and more fiery than the Portagee's guns.

Over dinner Isoke told the generals stories from the books of great battles and each battle's lesson, from Kadesh to the Siege of Dapur, from epic Pelusium to the heartbreak of Maggido. The soldiers of Nala gleaned how to use terrain to their advantage, and the value of triangulation, and the timing of collapsing flanks.

"Your Queen thanks you, Architect," said Nala when the Benin gathered to depart.

"What you have given me is more than what I gave you," replied Isoke.

"You have repaid me well. *Aht aht Acht aut.*"

"Such modesty," noted Simtho as the Queen's caravan disappeared into the horizon.

Isoke nodded.

She tapped her index finger at the edge of one eye.

She had already guessed what comes next.

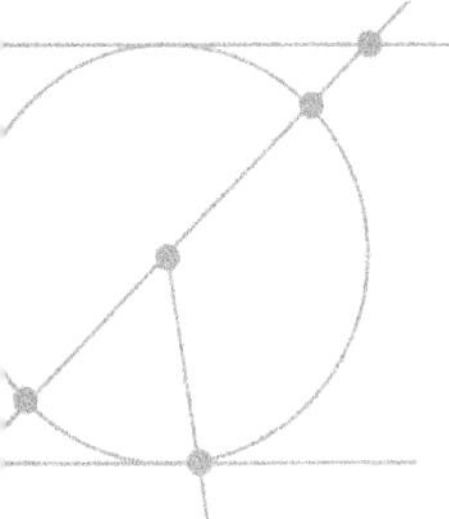

# POINTS ON A LINE

Every eleven years, the sun's magnetic field
reverses. No one knows why.
*-- Jacek Duka*

I SOKE, NOW THE ARCHITECT, MOSTLY THOUGHT NALA'S assassins would come from the west, for she knew Nala's limited understanding of maps, and landscapes.

She was correct.

Nala's predictable thought process produced a death-minded party of seven making its clumsy, noisy way through the tall grass by the hunting blinds, right where the migratory cat-paths lie. Celestial lights illuminated them as clearly as a small herd of elephants.

They seemed genuinely surprised to be caught.

The battle had been quick and clean and one-sided.

"This will change everything," said Osaharo.

Isoke chuffed in agreement.

She gripped the hilt of her long dagger reflexively, as though a lion had appeared in the shrubs.

We all wind our individual ways through the fairgrounds, pulling a weight, walking through a landscape of sights, sounds, songs and smells, goings-on beyond our understanding.

We see only parts of the whole.

Another flock of birds -- auks, this time – arched above the landscape in a collapsing-then-expanding cylinder action.

The omen did not pass unnoticed.

Isoke marked how the living funnel rose and sank three times.

To her brothers, she said:

"Nala dies."

Someone had to say it.

Simtho nodded. He drew in the dust with his toes.

"It can be no other way."

They watched Osahar roll the bones.

"I warned her not to come to Idiwekasi," Isoke reminded her brothers. "I warned her to leave us alone."

"Once Nala is gone, the people will want a new Queen," commented Ypiku.

"You, probably," agreed Osahar.

"We'll see," replied Isoke.

Isoke publicly executed three of Nala's assassins.

They allowed two others to swear allegiance and join their cadre (over Osahar's objections).

Isoke showed mercy on the royal counselor, Esigie, who had led the party. Isoke snapped both Esigie's arms and sent her back to Nala, as witness to what had just happened, and as herald for what was about to happen.

This proved to be a colossal mistake, for after the Night of Hyenas, Esigie fled Benin. She eventually allied with debauched Leb and the armies of the Xhosa to conquer the Kingdoms of the North. She then dedicated the entire span of her dynasty (as did her son, the smiler Eban) to erasing all traces of Isoke's geometries. The villainous pair did not rest until every shred of the Architect's work was purged from the lands of Benin and the histories of Africa in general, in word, song, structure and sculpture. Every last piece of the Architect's legacy would be burned and demolished.

Which is why you have never heard of her, nor have any, save the Navigators.

The Portagee would return, emerging out of the mists at the waterfalls at Wli, or Agumatsa, as some call it, waterfalls which are the gateway to lower Africa. He would ride at the head of a colonizing army, such a force as the Lands of the South had never seen.

He would not, however, reckon on the young German Navigator, Leo, to appear and to fight so valiantly at the Architect's side ...

But that is a tale for another day.

# TOM'S NOTES

GEOMETRY IS THE STUDY OF SPACE -- distance, shape, size, the relative position of figures -- and much more. Geometry is used in mapping, surveying, navigation, and astronomy. Geometry and arithmetic are among the oldest branches of mathematics (Number Theory is among of the newest). Advanced mathematicians use differential geometry to study problems involving curvature.

Galileo says that mathematics is the language of the natural world. It is a type of mathematics that, unlike other mathematics, is half-design. There are no equations, such as you find in algebra, or formulae, or algorithms. Geometry tracks mathematical patterns found in nature, such as tessellations and the Fibonacci sequence. It can help explain the way galaxies spiral, a seashell curves, patterns replicate, and rivers bend. For example, we can see a Fibonacci spiral in nature in the form of shells and the shape of hurricanes, even spirals in a pinecone.

One powerful concept springing from geometry is symmetry. I don't actually understand symmetry as it is studied in higher math, but I have a grasp of it in Frank Lloyd Wright's Imperial Hotel, and in a person's face, and in a butterfly. Audiences have problems with stories that break the law of symmetry – the villain's punishment at the end has to be the same volume and degree as the hero's suffering in the beginning.

Another such concept is triangulation. You will find it in politics, in family dynamics or group dynamics in general. Soccer and basketball are largely based on moving triangles, the shapes changing with movement, re-forming in a new pattern with every heartbeat.

# Galileo wrote that the Book of Nature is "written in mathematical language, and its characters are triangles, circles and other geometric figures, without which it is impossible to humanly understand a word; without these, one is wandering in a dark labyrinth."

The golden ratio is a third mathematical idea that appears in geometry, as well as in art, nature, and architecture.

If there is mystery in mathematics (and there is), much of it resides in geometry.

I just made that up, but I think it's true. At least it's true for me. Of all the fields of mathematics, Geometry seems to me the best positioned to capture the complex systems of modern world. If we had such a thing as geometry glasses, we would see patterns not just in highway traffic and bee swarms but also in stock markets and earthquakes, patterns too subtle and kinetic for the rational mind to capture.

In this story, I wanted to find a way for my protagonist, Isoke, to access mathematics without her tapping into European books. I was not able to master African math in order to do so.

Isoke the Architect goes on to become the central character of the African Navigator saga, joining forces with a tribe of seeming idiots and dyslexic young Leo from *The Illustrated Colonials.*

# Yan Li
## and the

# NUMERATORS

In the summer of 1958, farm girl Yan Li is a
member of the mathematics team assembled
to plan the Great Leap Forward. What she
finds is far from 'great.'

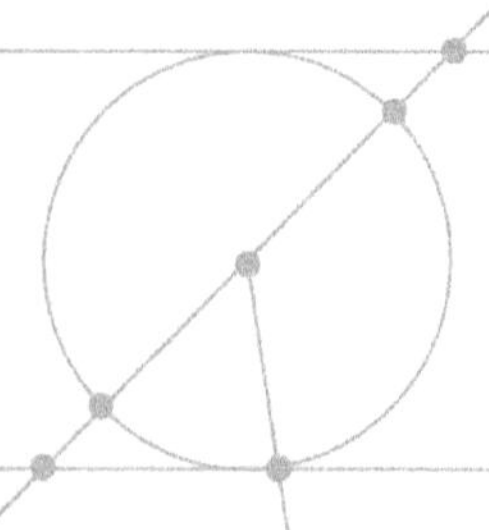

# A DISRUPTION ON THE COUNTING FLOOR

The Great Famine remains a taboo in China,
where it is referred to euphemistically as the
'Three Years of Natural Disasters' or the
'Three Years of Difficulties.'
-- *Tani Branigan, The Guardian*

FRECKLES, WELL-EARNED FROM WORKING LONG DAYS IN the sun, sprinkled the bridge of the nose and spilled over onto the cheeks of the face of the farm girl, Yan Li.

A badge of honor in her home region, the freckles were looked on as a relic of the agrarian past in certain sectors of modern China. The New China. Industrial China.

"Don't do this!" whispered Ming Jun, seated beside her. "The bridge bombing has everyone on edge. What if they --"

"Someone has to say something."

Yan Li's eyes were clear, her jaw firm, her expression determined. She straightened the barrette holding her hair back.

Yan Li stood up.

"Sit down!" hissed Ming Jun,

*"These mathematics are wrong! All wrong!"*

Yan Li announced this to the room full of working clerks and book-keeps on the expansive counting floor of Building Two.

Her voice was too loud to be ignored.

Faces turned towards her.

"It's all bad," she continued. "Completely phony. The assumptions are fabricated. You know this!"

The calm murmur of adding and multiplying, of calculations and quiet consultations, of pens scratching on paper, the soft clanking of typewriters in the half-walled stations which ringed the floor of low desks offices – all sounds on the counting floor subsided.

"A thousand times ridiculous is still ridiculous. I can't be the only one who thinks so."

Two of the red-kerchiefed floor proctors hustled towards Yan Li. After all, she was disrupting the entire society's forward progress.

"Sit back down, farm girl," commented one of her tallying peers. But the lone jibe froze in the air. None others joined.

"Look," said Yan Li evenly, "if anyone believes the se so-called *forecasts* we are producing ... well then, their deaths will be on our heads, comrades. It will be our fault if we do not speak up"

By now, even the soft plucking of stringed instruments in the background had fallen silent.

"We-cannot-possibly-endorse-this-charade!" concluded Yan Li.

"It's the millet," called out a second fellow scribe, a boy near the middle. "The winter wheat numbers are higher --"

"A FACTOR of FOUR higher?" demanded Yan Li. "The families who sit and wait for those phantom grains will be sorely disappointed, my friend. Empty bowls! They will starve and it will be *horrible* -- "

"Her work has been strenuous, Shi'lang," implored Ming Jun to the first proctor, "the hours long. Just let her sit back down."

"All right," said the proctor Shi'lang, a handsome older boy dressed in white with a red kerchief around his neck. "That's quite enough!"

"Who will join me in a new and honest set of calculations?" demanded Yan Li.

A loud knock on the glass walls.

A trio of the skinny soldiers, buck-toothed boys in green suits, rifles slung over shoulders, had paused in their campus patrol. Were they needed, to restore order?

Shi'lang waved them away.

Shi'lang draped an arm around Yan Li's shoulder and laughed in a most friendly fashion.

"Ah! Yes! Now I see the error you mention, Yan Li. I had noticed it, too. You are a prankster! Charming." He chuckled.

A little bell was ringing. It emanated from the corner office, raised above the count-ing floor. The Supervisor's office.

A second floor-proctor joined Shi'lang and together they ushered Yan Li off the floor.

"'Charade,'" laughed handsome Shi'lang, shaking his head wryly.

The members of the counting floor disliked this show of force.

Rumblings started up in the back rows …

Across the big open room, another red-bandana youth clapped his hands.

"Back to work, please."

The morning fruit and cheese platters were quickly circulated, an hour earlier than usual.

The soft plucking of lutes rose once again.

Gradually, unevenly, the Chairman's work continued.

# IN THE OFFICE OF THE SUPERVISOR

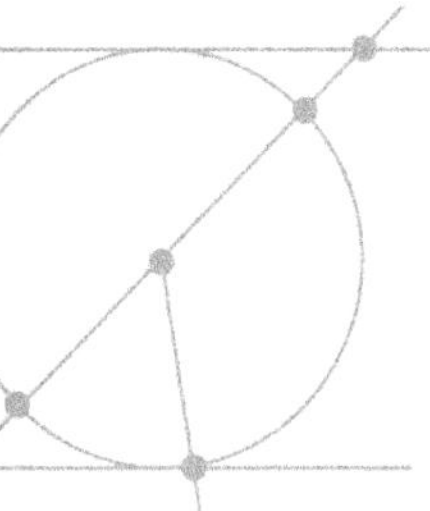

By the end of the first millennium A.D., China
possessed a sophistication in the technology
of traditional agriculture that has never been
surpassed ... the basic contours of this spectacular
agricultural system were laid during the
Classical period.
*– Agriculture in Ancient China*

THE CHAIRMAN'S SUMMER VILLA COMPOUND IN MEI LING is most pleasant.
Dappled sunlight graces the secluded retreat, a well-manicured place most
conducive to quiet contemplation and deep thoughts.  Burbling streams and winding
paths run through the sylvan grounds of the lakeshore campus. Mountain goats roam
the cliffs and munch on grass at the forested margins. Staircases and antique cable
cars bring visitors down the sharp inclines leading to Lake Wuhan at the compound's
western edge.  Deer stoop to drink from still ponds by Building Four.

Red drapes frame tableaus of blond furniture and upholstered chairs of the lobbies
within the glass walls of Building Three. An assembly hall could be glimpsed beyond
the plum carpeting.

Among the tall pine and bamboo trees, the young soldiers with their guard dogs
walked the paths winding up to bulky Building One. A swimming pool was hidden
behind its tinted windows.  Building Two, where the agricultural forecasts in support
of the coming Great Leap Forward – the bold initiative which would establish and

a new China -- were taking place, where Yan Li had created such a commotion, was lower and sleeker.

The star-splashed freckles sprinkled across Yan Li's nose and cheeks stood out now. Her blood was rising, and the skin of her face was flushed with anger.

The Supervisor, Miss Wang Na, paced the striped rug of the corner office. She paused to look out over the clerks working on their calculations o forecast the coming harvests.

Yan Li stood, defiant. Her hands had been tied.

Cushions in primary colors decorated the white sofas in the glass-walled office. Ivory rugs offset a row of wood-paneled bookshelves behind the large desk.

"We have summoned the Director," said Miss Wang Na.

"He left for Xinhua an hour ago, but we can get him back."

She paced behind metal standing lamps.

"Summon Empress Lu *Zhi* and the Seven Hoardes of *Han* for all I care," commented Yan Li.

"This is most serious," said Shi'lang

Miss Wang Na paused to consider the lake.

The glass corner office was perched on and above sparkling blue Lake Wuhan's shoreline. Splashing paddle-boats and brightly colored lanterns strung along the lake-side walkways gave no hint as to what might lay beneath the deep waters' surface.

Miss Wang Na turned, cursing bitterly.

"First the bombing! Then the Yunhe rebels attack our supply lines. Now this! Treason from within!"

"You're the traitor!" spat Yan Li. "You are complicit in what will be a famine of colossal proportions! Death by starvation.  In the millions -- "

"Why are you trying to make me look bad, farm girl?" demanded Miss Wang Na.

"To save tens of thousands of lives," answered Yan Li.

"The Director will be presenting our tables to the Bureau, in Beijing, in less than a week. If the net present values do not align -- "

"Oh, that part is easy enough," refuted the girl. "The net present value of next year's famine is 'Famine.' Also known as 'Zero.'"

"Yes, well, your barn-yard stubbornness, your backward ways, your slavery to tradition, your LACK of VISION are exactly what the Chairman fears most. I was present during his address at the Beijing Palace, and he predicted that these epochal events woul -- "

"Setting bad mathematics in historical context doesn't change anything," said Yan Li.

"Reactionary." Shi'lang shook his head. "*Confucian.*"

"'Confucian'? It's not *Confucian*. The calculations need to be exact. Based on reality. It all must be *intentional*. Not some empty exercise. If the numbers are compromised even slightly, it's all worthless. No forecast. How can you not see that?"

The net present value of next year's famine is 'Famine.' Also known as 'Zero.'

"Oh, I see," said the Supervisor, Miss Wang Na.

"I see, all right."

"What's this? Eh?" asked the Supervisor sharply.

She pointed to the equation at the top of one of Yan Li's pages.

"What is the meaning of this formula?"

$$\text{Yield in t/ha} = (220 \times 24 \times 3.4) / 10{,}000 = 1.79$$

"It's not a formula," answered Yan Li, shaking her head. "It's an equation.

"It shows the crop yield in any given harvest. Every forecaster follows this same model."

"And why is it incomplete?" demanded the Supervisor.

"It's waiting for a proper numerator. What you gave me is garbage. Worse than garbage."

Shi'lang moved as if to strike her. Miss Wang Na stepped between them.

"Let X equal X," challenged Yan Li, stepping forward --

"What does that mean?" demanded Miss Wang Na.

There was a pounding on the glass wall.

Again, the skinny, buck-toothed boys in green uniforms – a different group this time -- wanted to know if their services could be of use.  Again, Shi'lang shooed them away

"Show me the numerator," demanded Yan Li.

"What?"

"Show me where you got those numerators, bandana-boy. The supposed crop harvests for the next three years. The yields. The models, to be spread over the districts. From whence are they derived?"

"I have no patience with this double-talk," replied Shi'lang.

"You MADE THEM UP, that's why you can't show me-- "

"We factored in accelerated production rates for the new collectives," said Shi'lang, calming himself. "Of course we did. And these are many times the yield of privately-owned farmland.  Lysenko's models prove it -- "

"Lysenko," commented Yan Li with sarcasm bordering on contempt.

"Are you a farmer?" Yan Li asked.

Handsome Shi'lang glared at her.

"Answer my question.

"Brother, our honest argument benefits the Chairman's plan, surely. If you can prove me wrong, I will go back to my seat. Gladly so.

"Have you ever worked on an actual farm? Have you ever seen with your own two eyes yields of this magnitude? An acre of soil is not a factory floor!  You can't just wave a magic pencil -- "

"I know that! The forecasts worry me, too."

The Supervisor swiveled her head on her neck to regard handsome Shi'lang, This comment was unexpected.

Both Yan Li and the proctor, Shi'lang, brooded. They were alike, in some ways.

"The Director will soon deal with you," said Miss Wang Na. "He is not so nice as me.

"He has been known to torture counter-revolutionaries. Like you ...

"Ah! Here he comes now -- "

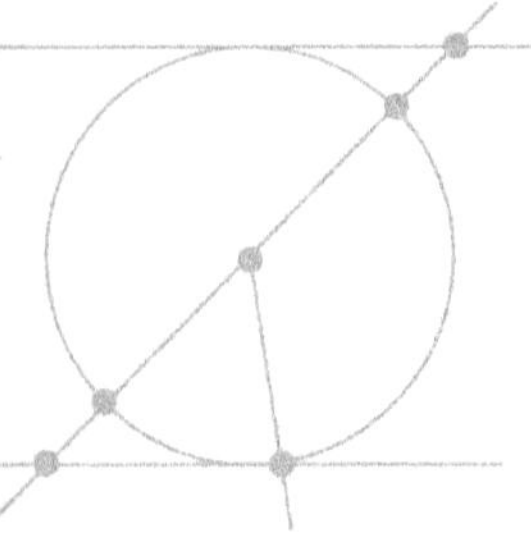

# THE DIRECTOR

If two is ten, then one would be nine,
and zero would be eight. This looks bad.
It looks like we broke mathematics.
– *Dan Finkel*

THE PROPER DISTANCE BETWEEN ROWS OF TOMATO plantings were regularly discussed in the halls of Emperor Yao, among the Hemudu leaders of Yuoyang, and many more.

For millennia, stretching back to the days of Yan, the first emperor, and Houji of the Zhou clan, the methods and techniques of agronomy were the Cathay leaders' highest priority. Each empire must first feed its populace, and always act to see them through the inevitable hard times. Great care was taken by the regional ministries to set aside stores of grain for lean years. The Yunhe Canal masters registered crop yields, and manage d store-houses in accordance with the almanacs. All sane mammals hoard food during the sunny times so they can live through the dark times. It is in our nature.

But in the newly created Kingdoms of Zhonhua, in the People's Republic, in the new order, in the year 1958, times had changed.

A new directive had been declared by the Chairman and a dozen or so despotic men in collared jackets. It changed everything. The state would transform China with coal-fired smokestacks. China would leap from the feudal ages into the modern world, a Great Leap Forward. Factories and highways and gleaming cities would be built at breakneck speed, at the expense of tillers and gardeners and orchards.

Those who stood in the way would be promptly murdered.

The Director, Dao Xiang Qi, a tall and imposing young man, scowled.

A shock of hair hung over his forehead as he flipped through the pages of Yan Li's notes. The Supervisor, Miss Wang Na, narrated the morning's events.

"What do you have to say for yourself, young lady?" the Director challenged Yan Li.

"I have this to say," retorted Yan Li. "Unless you have stashed TEN MILLION TONS of soybeans that I am unaware of, there's going to be hell to pay in the provinces of China come next June.

"And the harvest after that will bring back the days of Huang Chao!"

This particular reference disturbed even Miss Wang Na, for it introduced the idea of famine-sparked rebellion.

"All right. That's enough."

The Director stood. He motioned for the guards to open the door.

"You haven't heard me out -- " protested  Yan Li.

"There is no need," replied Dao Xiang Qi coldly.

"This."

The Director gestured with his hands, towards the counting floor.

"What has happened here today.

"It began as honest inquiry. A point of clarification.

"But the moment you stood up, and halted work among the citizens, it became insurrection."

Miss Wang Na smoothed either sleeve of her sweater. She had done the right thing, after all.

"I have cancelled my trip to the Assembly in Xinhua," continued the Director. "Two Prefects are on their way as we speak. The investigation will begin first thing tomorrow.

"You seem sincere," the Director told Yan Li. "It will be taken into account. "But whatever you thought you were doing ... we have strict procedures -- "

"I tried to tell you -- " interjected Shi'lang

"Once the apparatus is set into motion …" The Director did not feel required to complete the sentence.

"Come with me," the Director told Yan Li, somehow making three words sound like an extended threat.

"Bring your notes."

"Keep walking," said the Director under his breath once they were outside, moving briskly along the gravel pathway.

"Don't look up."

He surreptitiously untied her hands. They headed across the campus, northward, towards the parking lots.

"I am part of a splinter group," he told her. "Farmers, rebels, good men and women. We all know that urgent action is needed.

"We have to hurry. Another bomb is set to go off."

Now a figure approached on the pathway from Building Four. It was a tall girl. She was in a hurry.

They turned and headed on a path northward, parallel to the lake shore.

"The Yunhe have nothing to do with our efforts. The Yunhe transport us but stay aloof, old maids that they are. We will get your calculations to Gua Qin, she will-- "

A sudden detonation – impossibly loud – shook the calm air of the retreat.  The blast shivered the trees with its force. The explosion came from the far side of Building Four.

Smoke rose over the roofline --

A second bomb exploded, the dull thud of its concussion shaking the earth beneath their feet.

The girl coming towards them broke into a run--

"Here is my niece," said the Director.

"Slow down, cousin …"

"The road is blocked," the Niece hissed. "This way!"

She led them directly towards the cliffs.

"A boat is waiting – down the stairs -- "

A nearby gaggle of the green-suited guards had noticed the girl's haste.

"Halt! Halt there!" their leader called out – cautiously, at first, then with command as they ignored him --

The patrol raced towards them --

The trio reached the chain fence gate entrance to the stairs. The Director burst through with a kick, rattling the locks.

A waterfall spilled down the gorge, kicking up mist.

The staircase down to the lake had been chiseled into the cliffs

Alongside was an antique cable-car, an old-fashioned funicular, a suspended tram on pulley and ropes where the two cars are connected, so that one can only rise if the other falls.

They descended into the water-splashed gorge on slippery stone steps, clutching the railings.

Across the gorge, Yan Li glimpsed the figures of Shi'lang and Miss Wang Na, watching from a balcony in front of the glass walls of Building Two.

The Proctor carried a rifle.

In the Supervisor's right hand was gripped the unmistakable contour of a Mauser C96 handgun.

"Don't fire!!" Yan Li called.

The patrol-boys clattered through the gate behind them --

One of them grabbed Yan Li's collar

She swiveled her shoulders to sweep his hand away.

Scooping the rifle from his shoulder, Yan Li flung the boy off the staircase. He toppled, squawking in surprise, and fell into the waters below --

Now bullets pinged around her, bouncing off the stone cliffs --

One struck the Director.

He grunted and spun half-around with impact.

The Niece caught him.

Yan Li looked up –

It was Shi'Lang and Miss Wang Na firing down on them.

The Proctor bolted his rifle for another shot --

Yan Li instantly raised the rifle she had taken from the green-suited boy --

It was one of the Type 24 rifles, a Generalissimo, and she hefted it like it was an old friend.

She let loose two quick rounds.

The shots made crisp, cracking sounds. The reports echoed off the gorge walls.

Two figures fell from the balcony --

Yan Li fired all five rounds in the clip to dissuade the green suits clambering downward after her --

Now they reached a platform beside the open door to one of the cable cars. They leapt in --

Bullets pinged off the tram car's metal casement --

Yan Li pulled the cord at the front of the tram.

The ropes and pulleys creaked –

She tried harder, using all the torque and leverage she could muster. Her hands burned.

The heavy car would not budge

She hopped twice and yanked down with all her might.

Something in her shoulder snapped --

She pulled still harder.

*If I'm going to die, it won't be trapped like a rodent.*

Slowly, the tram moved, quickly picking up speed –

Two minutes later, the two girls emerged onto the little lakeside dock, dragging a hobbled Dao Xiang Qi.

The pilot helped them clamber into the waiting motorboat.

They heard confused shouting behind them, calling back and forth as the boat pulled away.  One voice shouted that the Director had been taken hostage ...

The motorboat revved.

Yan Li felt the boat advance, straining towards the lake's central expanse, as though it were trying to rise above the grasping waters which held it back.

Seen close-up, the skin on her face was covered in a layer of red.

The towel wiped away blood from the nose and skin of Yan Li's features.

One more swipe of the towel...

The freckles emerged.

"There we go," said the Niece. She turned Yan Li's face left and right, inspecting for wounds. She grunted. No cut. The blood had come from the Director's wound.

The loud sound of multiple motors filled the air.

The boat kicked up a high wake, like a rooster's crown, as they sped away from the shores. It was a Lone Star GC 600, one of the handsome but heavy wooden-hull boats, wide-beamed, American, modified with extra horsepower. No pursuing vessel, no flotilla on this lake or on the entire length of the Grand Canal could overtake it.

"Your shoulder is dislocated." The Niece took hold of Yan Li's forearm and turned it back and forth, as though taking measure – with a yank, she corrected the joint. Yan Li winced and gave a muffled shout.

Now the Niece turned her attention to Dao Xiang Qi.

"It's not as bad as I thought," she called over the sounds of motors. Deftly she removed the bandage and replaced it with a clean one. The pale-faced Director sank back in the seat-cushion. He closed his eyes.

Yan Li blinked. She looked around. The Lake was rimmed by the cottages and vacation homes of the Politburo. She glimpsed gay pavilions and paddle boats, red buoys and strings of channel markers, leisure-time dinghies and sailboats.

"Can I see my family?" Yan Li asked the Niece.

The Niece looked back at Yan Li.

Yan Li knew the answer. Her home was a long way west, and the boat was headed south.

Towards Shanghai.

A tidal wave was coming.

She had been called from the sidelines to play her part in the grand drama that was about to unfold in the Lands of Cathay.

The game had begun.

She gripped the metal support.

Her eyes swept the shoreline as the boat made its broad turn into a section above one of the ancient lake's cavernous gorges. Far, far below them sat silent open-jawed fossils facing upward along the floors of submerged chasms and shock-changed quartz, canyons gaping below looming lateral spans of limestone and granite, witnesses to a now-drowned Triassic empire, a fractured, glacier-driven terrain.

Yan Li would soon see for herself what deep waters were like.

These would be fathoms deep.

A terrible famine was coming.

China needed her.

# TOM'S NOTES

WHILE THE HISTORY OF IT HAS BEEN suppressed in the East and remained unknown in the West, China's famine of 1958-1962 represents one of the worst man-made calamities in modern history. Recent estimates place the figure at 36 million deaths – and the majority were preventable.

Estimates vary. Many historical researchers believe even this incomprehensible figure might be too low, due to government under-reporting.  While the rest of the world's attention was distracted by Sputnik 3, hula hoops, and Sir Edmund Hilary reaching the South Pole, a man-made calamity worse than the Black Plague was unfolding behind an opaque wall of silence, in Communist China. Mao Tse-tung's irrational policy  veered radical off course. Here is an account from a Xinhua reporter named Lu Baoguo that gives a narrow window into what must have been an unimaginable and vast landscape of horrors:

> *In the second half of 1959, I took a long-distance bus from Xinyang to Luoshan and Gushi. Out of the window, I saw one corpse after another in the ditches. On the bus, no one dared to mention the dead. In one county, Guangshan, one-third of the people had died.*

In his excellent book, "Tombstone: The Great Chinese Famine 1958-1962," journalist Yang Jisheng gives us a chilling tapestry of these events.

What happened to cause the Great Famine? I don't know, but one factor was that Mao wiped out all of his critics. His abstract planning suffered from a lack of more realistic counter-forces. A healthy opposition – both a rival political party and a free press -- makes for a vigorous government. In his excellent book, "Tombstone," Yang Jisheng documents both his family's tragedy and the China catastrophe.

The figures which drove the Great Leap Forward were fiction, according to Yang Jisheng's reporting. He uncovered a document written by Xue Muqiao, former head of the national statistics bureau, in 1958 that stated, "we give whatever figures the upper-level wants," to overstate disasters and relieve official responsibility for deaths due to starvation.

You and I need to learn everything we can know about this. Thirty-five million people cannot die without making a ripple.

---

The mathematics of forecasting has to do with statistics and reading data and identifying numerical trends. It is an important part of the applied math of economics, that dark science which 'explains' the past much better than it predicts the future. A mastery of math provides you the tool to give shape to the wealth of data which surrounds us. The mathematics of probability may also lead you to game theory, which to me is both fascinating and elusive.

In my story, Yan Li is looking for all the components of true forecasting. She does not see data representing the many complementing factors which influence crops –

# Critics were purged in numbers that look fantastical ... Mao acknowledged that the Chinese government had killed 700,000 "counterrevolutionaries" between 1950 and 1952.

*--Gilbert King*

humidity, soil, weather, etc. It was more than the math at fault, since the entire Great Leap Forward initiative depended on duplicity.

I urge you to acquire the skills of reading data. I have several helpful link s posted on the Mathgirls.com website. All around you, companies are collecting and interpreting your own data. Google knows when the flu is coming to Seattle because they see the increase in cough syrup consumption tracking northward from San Francisco to Portland. You want that kind of data-based wisdom.

The Middle Kingdom's tradition of careful food storage and agricultural management referred to in 'Numerators' is for real. "By the end of the first millennium A.D.," Robert Eno writes in Agriculture in Ancient China, "China possessed a sophistication in the technology of traditional agriculture that has never been surpassed ... the basic contours of this spectacular agricultural system were laid during the Classical period."

"Vegetables were planted in garden plots," wrote Ban Gu, "and at the borders of living and working areas were planted melons and gourds, fruit trees and cucumber. Chickens, pigs, dogs, and swine were raised for food with close attention to their timely needs."

To position the empire against the Xiongnu, invaders from the north, agro-colonies of crops for the military were formed in the border regions, to support imperial garrisons.

All this care for agronomy makes the Great Famine of 1958-62 all that much more tragic. Mao unveiled the Great Leap Forward at a meeting in January, 1958, in Nanjing. It was an abstraction, a plan, concocted in offices, to bring China into the modern world, alongside Europe and America.  The central idea was that rapid development of China's agricultural and industrial sectors should take place in parallel ... yet industry was favored, at the expense of the traditional apparatus of food storage and management.

The Great Leap Forward swept aside the traditional respect for agronomy and this diligent preparation for seventh-year famines. It proved to be beyond calamitous for the people of China. Its consequences still echo today, and now surely represents the burial ground for a treasure of untold stories.

Writing these stories was easier than usual for me because I felt that in each case there was a story waiting to be told. I did not need some genius description or brilliant plot twist. I could just prop my cast of characters against the tidal wave and let the story tell itself. I took it as a good sign that I enjoyed Yan Li's deadly revenge on Miss Wang Na and the Proctor Shi'lang so very much. I can't wait for the big story yet to come, in which Yan Li becomes a national heroine, moving through fields of

# In sowing crops, there was always a mix of the five major grains in order to guard against blights affecting one grain. Ploughing was done with energy and the fields were frequently weeded; the harvest was reaped as though bandits were about to appear. Encircling the cottages, mulberry trees were planted.

*--Treatise on Food and Money"*
*by Ban Gu, 1st century A.D.*

death like a living being among zombies to save her countrymen from famine and autocrats, both regional and central.

I have once again made use of the fictional Yunhe – my heroic family of Grand Canal caretakers – and the shadowy Navigators in order to bolster my story structure. More about them can be gleaned in my previous historical fiction, particularly The Illustrated Colonials and King James' Seventh Company, as well as in stories yet to come.

# Shawnee
## and the
# VISITOR

An enterprising student economist in Florida
of 1967 shows Martin Luther King and Bayard
Rustin something to change their way
of thinking.

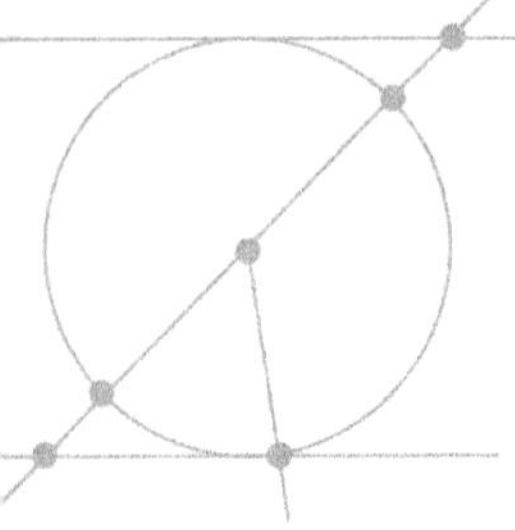

# PROLOGUE

We have little trouble remembering the Rev.
Martin Luther King Jr. as a civil rights icon. But
we rarely do the harder work of remembering
the full King ... We particularly fail to remember
his call for Americans to do something hard but
necessary: redistribute wealth.
*-- Douglas E. Thompson*

CISSY SAW THE LIGHT IN SHAWNEE'S WINDOW.

She opened her own window and leaned out into the moonlight

"You need to get some sleep, young lady," she called out in a stage whisper.
"Tomorrow's gonna be a big day."

The two women, twenty years apart in age, were best of friends.

Shawnee's father and Cissy's husband had long ago given up trying to keep them
apart.

"I lost it," whispered her neighbor, young Shawnee Smith.  Shawnee leaned
forward, balancing her weight on her own window sill.

"I was rehearsing. For tomorrow. And now I can't find it. The necklace," she whispered. "The one Ma gave me."

"You lose that thing three times a day," assured her friend.  "It'll turn up.
Always does."

Cissy climbed through her own window and onto the big branch and down the trellis. She picked her way carefully through the garden, then clambered easily into her neighbor's second-story window.

"When's Tug get back?" asked Shawnee.

She was sitting on the bed, in her bathrobe. Her legs were still in the braces. The wheelchair sat patiently, clothes draped over it, within arm's length.

"Supposed to be Saturday," answered Cissy. "I just hope those Interceptors don't get into trouble over there …

"Can't sleep, thinking about it. The world, these days …"

Shawnee nodded. She worried just the same over her father's deployments.

Cissy looked under the bed for the necklace.

"What if the Reverend doesn't show tomorrow," asked Shawnee.

"You can't think like that," urged Cissy. "Think positive!"

"Okay," she told her friend.

"Watch this, Cis -- "

Shawnee moved her weight forward and, masking the effort it took, stood up.

"Thank you for coming today … " she said in the voice of a television hostess.

Her legs began to shake.

She adjusted the leather straps at the knee of one leg brace. The pins would not behave. She cursed bitterly.

"Oh no, now, young lady. None of that -- " Cissy admonished.

She moved to help with the braces. Shawnee swatted her hand away.

Shawnee hated help.

The teenager fixed the braces.

She practiced rising, graciously, from the bed, then she tried it from the wheelchair.

She practiced raising her hands naturally, as a teacher might do, or an eminent lecturer might do, without even thinking.

She stopped.

Shawnee sat down.

"He's not coming, is he?"

"You're just upset about the necklace," said Cissy. "We'll find it!"

The warmth and encouragement in her voice were unforced, quiet, persistent. The two had an understanding.

# ON TALLAHASSEE STREET



THE HOUSING UNITS FOR TYNDALL AIR FORCE Base, the Florida panhandle home to the 325th Operations Group, were well-equipped with dishwashers and refrigerators and televisions and air conditioning – all the modern conveniences promised in the World War.

On an E-5 salary, Staff Sergeant Saginaw Smith, valued member of the Second Fighter Interceptor Squadron, had provided well for his family.

Right now, the Sergeant stood at the bay window in the carpeted living room of his home. He was using a military-issue pair of binoculars, leather lash around his neck, to scan the street and, beyond, the flat Florida vista.

"Quit watching, Daddy. Come have a lemonade."

Jimmy Davis and the Twibell boys were playing street hockey out front. Several neighborhood girls on bicycles circled the action. One of them was singing that old song, "At the Hop."

"Two hours late," he chided. "These big-city Negroes ..."

"They're not coming," said Shawnee. "I'm almost happy. I've been all nervous about it anyway."

"Hold your horses now, girl. Here's someone ... "

A '62 Chevrolet Bel Air approached, turning onto Tallahassee Street. The car drove past the youth center, slowed down for the hockey game, and kept going past the Smith household.

"Nope," said the Sergeant.

Shawnee and Cissy played cards without enthusiasm in the dining room.

The card game changed from Crazy Eights to Slap Jack.

The distinctive drone of a fighter rose from outside. Torquing engines grew from a background noise to a roar, right overhead.

"F-84 Escorts," called the Sergeant. "Big shots. Too slow for the damn MIGS, though. Those swept wings ..."

Now he saw two 1958 Plymouth Club Coupes, big and clunky and ugly, making their way up Tallahassee Street. .

The duo cruised cautiously up the street. They stopped to ask directions from Jimmy Davis. He pointed to the Smith house.

The two cars approached slowly.

The tires crunched gravel as they turned into the Smith driveway.

"Our guests have arrived," the Sergeant announced.

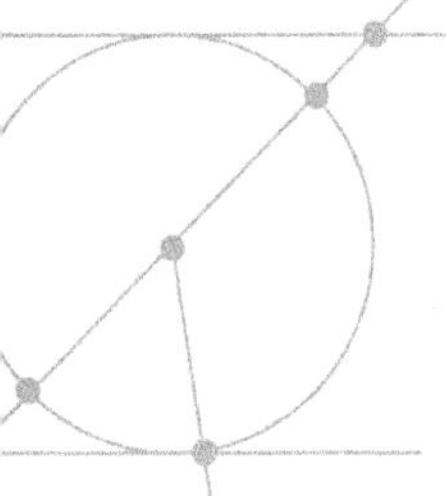

# LEMONADE

The best idea always wins.
*-- Matthew Weiner*

FOUR NEGRO MEN AND TWO NEGRO WOMEN stepped through the screen door and into the carpeted living room.  Heads bobbed and hands shook.

Sergeant Smith held the screen door open as they entered.

"Come on in.

"Master Sergeant Saginaw Smith, Second Fighter Squadron," Shawnee's father said.

"This here is my neighbor, Cissy Thomas."

Introductions were made.

"And this here is my daughter. Shawnee. She's the one you come to see ..."

In the center of the living room... sat a composed girl, all of fourteen.

She rose from her wheelchair and balanced on the leg braces.

Gawky on the way up, she stood tall and straight.

One of the women stepped forward. "Margery Rustin."

"Shawnee," said Margery Rustin. "We have come a long way to meet you."

Cissy handed out glasses of lemonade from two silver trays. She held a napkin in one hand to wipe away the beads of moisture that formed on the glasses and the pitcher and the tray itself.

"Martin," said Margery Rustin.

The others stepped aside to make way.

A man in his late thirties stepped forward.

He wore a dark suit, despite the summer heat. He held a hat in his left hand.

He extended his right hand.

"Martin Luther King, Jr., Miss Smith. Very pleased to meet you." His eyes were wide-set and kind. His voice was resonant.

Shawnee could not curtsy, or even bow, not much anyway, without risking her posture, with her leg-braces and crutches and all.

So she nodded her head in a most welcoming manner.

She shook hands warmly with her guest.

The quality of the girl's smile upon holding the hand of the Reverend King made all else suddenly secondary.

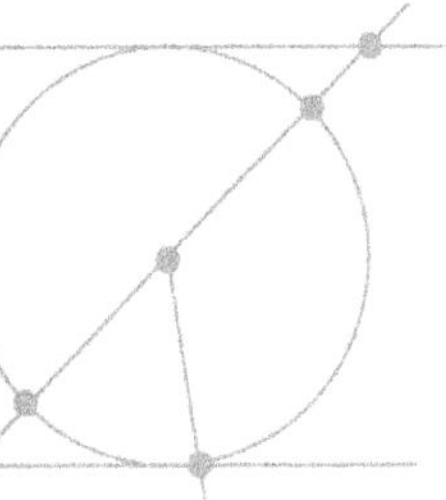

# THE CHALLENGE

Gold is its own country.

*-- Matthew Hart*

"**P**ROFESSOR JAMISON OF FLORIDA ATLANTIC SPEAKS so highly of you, Shawnee," said Margery Rustin when they were all seated.

"He urged us to make time. He seemed most genuine."

A heavy-set man, Jules Telford, sat forward on the green stiffed chair where the Sergeant often sat.

Glasses of lemonade were refilled from the pitcher on the silver platter.

"We detoured from Miami.

"We are anxious to learn of this mysterious equation in your letter.

$$GNNP = pop. \ (@11\%) \ @11\% + capital \ growth \% - OC$$

"And what you meant by the phrase 'Gross Negro National Product.'"

Shawnee set aside her notes.

"Yes, ma'am. I mean the Black American economy. Its dimensions and its changing nature, year over year."

"You have calculated that?"

"Yessir. You'll see the charts. And we believe we have a method to dramatically increase that number."

Jules Telford grunted.

The fan overhead whirred quietly, augmenting the hard-working air conditioning unit in the window.

"It's just that you all have worked so faithfully," continued Shawnee, "to gain rights from Congress for our people, when the truth is," she took a napkin to swipe beads of moisture which had appeared on the silver platter.

"The truth is that the Negro Nation," she said, "does not need any help. We can do fine on our own. Economically."

She smoothed her skirt.

Her father nodded his head.

"Mine is a *mighty* God," said Cissy softly, crushing the napkin in her hand.

# THE MODEL

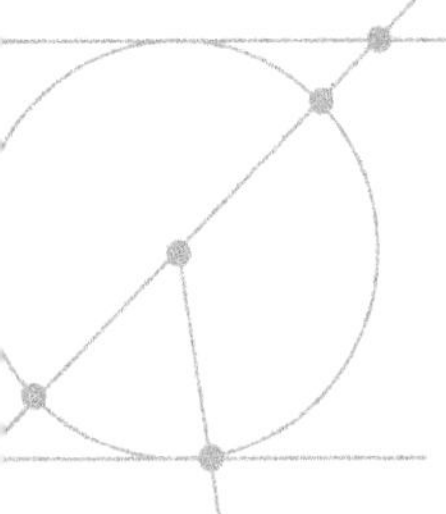

The poor themselves can create a poverty-free
world. All we have to do is to free them from the
chains that we have put around them!
-- *Muhammad Yunus*

"WE DON'T NEED AN ACT OF CONGRESS," said Shawnee Smith, the girl in leg braces.

Cissy methodically smoothed the wrinkled paper napkins on the coffee table as she listened.

"We don't need anybody. Or anything."

"Please tell us how you think such a thing is possible," urged Philip Randolph, on the edge of powerful emotions.

"Yessir."

The Smith home was one of those open floor plans, where a kitchen counter is all that divides the living room from the kitchen, the dining room being the open third space, adjacent to both.

"An Englishwoman," she began, "named Priscilla Wakefield. In 1779, she established a lending institution for poor children.

"Lending money to the poorest of the poor."

Sergeant Smith walked from the living room to the dining room, almost pacing.

"A bank for the poor," said Bayard Rustin.

"Yessir.  And only loaning to females," continued Shawnee. "Women lending to other women. Sometimes girls."

Marge Rustin chuckled.

"Nine dollars to start a bicycle repair shop. Seven dollars for a sewing machine. Twenty to dig a water well for the village.

"This bank had a repayment rate of 97%.

"It was hugely successful," said Shawnee. "The bank transformed village life."

"Interesting," said Bayard Rustin, making no effort to hide his disappointment.

"You brought us here, a day out of our way, to give us a *history* lesson ... "

He hitched up his trousers as a prelude to rising and departing, shooting a dark look at Margery for wasting their time --

"*Tell 'em,*" came the Sergeant 's voice from the dining room.

"So," continued Shawnee, "I took my own savings and tried it.

"I opened such a bank. Right here. In Callaway."

She plopped a financial report on the table, by the lemonade tray.

Rustin sat back down.

Philip Randolph took up the report.

Reverend King refilled his glass of lemonade.

A soft laugh could be heard from the dining room.

---

"Wait," said Margery Rustin. "You're saying that you yourself have tried this same thing?"

"Yes, ma'am. Eighteen months now. Our church. North Star Church. I'm the bank's president and chief financial officer.

"I started with ninety dollars. From my late Mother's will.

"Current cash assets: 17,981 dollars and 22 cents."

The silence in the room deepened. From the kitchen came the sound of the Frigidaire plopping ice cubes into a glass.

"And another fourteen thousand in equity," continued Shawnee.

"And we bought a piece of land ..."

Jimmy Davis and the boys paused playing street hockey to let a station wagon pass. Two of the group took up the chorus of "At the Hop."

Shawnee took a long drink of lemonade.

She made adjustments to the knee of a leg brace.

"Land?" asked Margery Rustin. Randolph and Reverend King exchanged looks.

"Yes, ma'am. The old cannery.

"The building's all but collapsed, but the plot is twelve acres. The assessor has a high opinion ..."

"And the town council gave us the zoning we need," added Cissy. "Shawnee explained it to them."

Telford gave a low whistle.

Philip Randolph and Bayard Rustin stood to remove their jackets. They draped them carefully over the chair backs.

Excusing herself, Shawnee used her crutches to make her way to the kitchen.

"She gets a little tired," explained Cissy. "Blood sugar and all. She makes herself peanut butter and jelly.

"If anyone wants one, there's plenty."

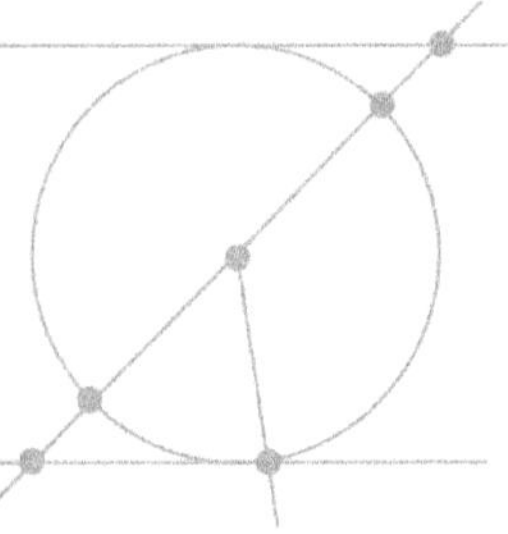

# INTERROGATION

Microfinance stands as one of the most promising
and cost-effective tools in the fight against global
poverty.
– *Jonathan Morduch*

"**H**EAR THAT?" ASKED SERGEANT SAGINAW SMITH AS the guests read through the folders.

He stood and walked to the window.

A heavy, massive sound in the sky above Tallahassee Street was coming closer, growing louder.

"Those are radial engines ... "

He picked up the binoculars resting on the table by the bay window.

"Superfortress. Boeing B-50. We got three of 'em ... "

"Now, young lady," said Bayard Rustin, raising his eyeglasses to his forehead.

"I've got a few questions --

"What interest rate do you charge?"

"None," answered Shawnee.

"She means it's voluntary," explained Cissy. "Each woman pays the interest she thinks is fair. The average is 9 per cent."

"Median or mean?"

"Median. The mean interest rate is 10.3 per cent."

"Defaults? Asked Randolph.

"Less than 3 per cent."

"You mention 'equity' here, on page four..." said Ralph Bunche.

"Yessir. Several women have chosen to make the group their partner," replied Shawnee." They give us a percentage of their sales."

"Yes," said Beverly Randolph. "That makes sense. You are acting almost as a partner."

"And how is it taxed?" asked Rustin.

"As a church activity. The IRS views it as barter."

"Where did these come from?" He pointed to figures in a chart, on page 11 of the binder.

"That's a Markov chain.  I have inserted historic values for the projections."

"They seem most conservative," said Randolph. "Considering."

"Professor Jamison thinks so," answered Shawnee.

"And what has been your average ROI?"

"Weighted average, 12.2 %," answered Shawnee. "Mean, 7.5%."

"That's quarterly," added Cissy, with some emphasis.

"*Quarterly?*" Randolph jumped out of his seat.

"*Quarterly?*" repeated Margery Rustin. "Truly?"

Both Cissy and Shawnee nodded. Cissy reached across and turned Rustin's report to the page with that data. She had helped type it.

Rustin gave a low whistle.

"The best part is," added Cissy, frustrated that Shawnee was not bragging, "you already have the means to scale this nation-wide."

Blank faces looked at her.

"Churches," said Cissy. "All the black churches. It's a network. You already have a national network in place. Willing hands. Free labor. And the plan is proven."

She refilled two of the lemonade glasses, taking care not to drip on the typed reports.

"Here," said Shawnee politely, "I have contrasted the yield to the Negro people of opening twenty such banks to the raising the minimum wage. It's on ...

"Page twelve ..."Cissy completed the sentence.

Shawnee leaned over to turn a page and nearly toppled. She caught herself and shifted to the wheelchair.

"Per your speech, Reverend. Last April ... "

"Not even close," murmured Bunche.

"We can help ourselves," said Telford. "No act of Congress needed."

The window air conditioner revved to a higher gear.

"And the *righteous* will shine forth," commented Beverly Randolph to herself, adjusting the collar of her blouse.

She bowed her head.

"At thy *right* hand," she added.

In the kitchen, the Sergeant chuckled. Cool air continued to gush out of the silver stainless steel blower of the window air conditioner.

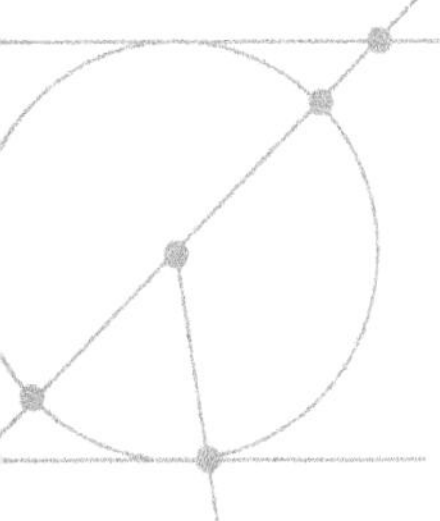

# CONCLUSION



*The original intent behind Martin Luther King
Jr.'s "I Have a Dream" speech was an appeal to end
economic and employment inequalities.*
*– Caleb Silver*

Martin Luther King, Jr. stood to address the group.

"I am a vain man," he said.

"I have fallen in love ...with the sound of my own voice."

"Yes," said Ralph Bunche.

"Yes, you have," agreed Rustin.

"And for all my vanity, all my speechifying, nothing has changed. Not really.

"Where are we today?

"Still begging for this law or that handout."

He shook his head at the thought.

"But this ..." He held up Shawnee's report. "This needs no speech.

"This needs no election. No favors.

"It is already ours."

"The Shawnee Smith Church Bank," laughed Margery.

"The Shawnee Smith Tiny Loan But Only to Females Financial Model," corrected Rustin.

"The Black Folks Bank," declared Ralph Bunche.

"The Black Folks Bank!!" agreed Martin with a laugh.

Amens all around.

Reports gripped, the men rose and draped their jackets over their arms.

The women helped return glasses and trays to the kitchen.

"We will have more questions," said Bunche to Shawnee with a nod. "We'll talk."

"Bless you, Shawnee."

Margery Rustin embraced the girl warmly, so that the crutches fell.

Margery picked them up.

Margery removed a silver chain from her own neck and showed it to Shawnee. The pendant on the necklace was black and white, with a tinge of green around the edges.

"Garnet is Martin's birth stone," explained Margery.

The initials "MLK" were embossed on the pearly white surface.

She hung it around Shawnee's neck and clasped it. She adjusted the necklace so that it looked like it always been there.

"Our next event is in Memphis. We are headed there now.

"We'll be staying at the Lorraine Motel.

"I will call you from there to report on our progress. I know Martin will want to act on this immediately -- "

Margery hugged Shawnee, long and close.

"I'm already making lists of churches -- " said Beverly as she opened the front door.

In the driveway, Sergeant Saginaw Smith handed a heavy dark green duffel bag to Ralph Bunche and Philip Randolph. The bag was marked '325th Operations Group.'

The two men looked inside the canvas bag to see military-grade Browning M19 rifles. The distinctive stocks were well-worn. "Full power." The Sergeant lifted one to show the bayonet clip. "That's a *battle* gun. Twenty rounds." These were serious guns, weapons of war, out of place in a suburban driveway.

"You don't even have to fire 'em," assured the Sergeant. "Just carry them around with you. Let them be seen.

"Lots of crazies out there. And not a one of them cares to be shot back at."

Ralph Bunche and Philip Randolph politely declined.

They shook his hand warmly.

The Twibell boys on their bikes, out in the street, made way. One of them pointed the cars towards the highway.

The two 1958 Plymouth Club Coupes pulled out and headed east on Tallahassee Street, to eventually turn right – north, that is -- on Highway 102.

Overhead, a squadron of Interceptors flew low, flat trajectories over the Florida panhandle.

"Sarge!" called Cissy from the living room.

"She's asking for you -- "

# TOM'S NOTES

MARTIN LUTHER KING PLACED GREAT EMPHASIS ON jobs. "Economics and economic history are usually neglected step-children at sessions on Civil Rights history," writes Gavin Wright in his 2006 paper, *The Economics of the Civil Rights Revolution*. He continues: "Expanding economic opportunity was an important motivation for the Civil Rights movement from its earliest days."

The Poor People's March on Washington was held in May 1968, but King's vision of ending poverty went largely unrealized. The economics of the civil rights era are of course still very much with us.

*Martin Luther King with Bayard Rustin (Wikimedia Commons)*

In the story, Shawnee is using techniques of forecasting – something you do already.

With mathematics we're able to show models for anything economically from micro (personal economics) to macro (large-scale economics, such as Gross Domestic Product, or GDP for short). These models can help you make better decisions in your own daily life, reducing uncertainty and anticipating change.

When you leave home without an umbrella, you are betting it won't rain. When you leave home at 7:15 and school starts at 8:00, you are forecasting traffic conditions.

Better life decisions can be made with mathematical models. For instance, it will certainly help you decide about going to college. Here is my fairly crude example:

You can get a job out of high school for $30,000 (Salary A). You are both earning money for four years and NOT spending money on tuition ($20,000 per year). Therefore, at first glance you are doing much better by NOT attending college.

Now run *all* the numbers.

Opportunity 1: NO COLLEGE

    4 years x salary A ($30,000) = a gain of $120,000

Opportunity 2: ATTENDING COLLEGE

    4 x no salary – tuition (20,000 per year x 4 years)
    0 - 80,000 = a loss of $80,000

Your opportunity cost of attending college after 4 years

    Missed salary plus tuition debt
    120,000 + 80,000
    200,000 (that is, a loss of $200,000)

But now you add in the critical part -- the next 10 years.

    10 years x salary B ($70,000) = $700,00

    $700,000 – opportunity cost of $200,000

    $500,000

You are $500,000 ahead if you attend college. The numbers clearly forecast that college is a long-term benefit.

This is an example of a term Shawnee and her accomplice  Cissy mention in the story: "ROI" is one the most telling ratios of all – *Return on Investment*.  Profit minus cost, divided by cost. You need to calculate yours.

The basic math of banks is as follows: take in deposits and pay interest of 1%, while lending out money at 4%. The delta – the difference – is what makes banking a viable industry.

You, reader, need to understand how economics work, both in your own life and career and in the national and world marketplaces around you. You have a balance sheet. You have an opportunity cost.

The clearest model for the Village financing approach is of course the Grameen Bank, a community development bank founded in Bangladesh which makes small loans (known as microcredit) to the impoverished. Its micro-loan program, a groundbreaking enterprise, was awarded a Nobel Prize in 2006.

The inclusion of Philp Randolph in the entourage that day in 1967 was not accidental. Randolph was one of the civil right movement leaders who stressed economics as a tent pole of true equality.

The character of Margery Rustin is fictional.

The idea of black banking and black economic self-development in this story exist in a larger context. Thomas Sowell is one economist who has written about this controversial topic. One issue is that governmental help for the impoverished (such as welfare programs) may tend to backfire. A second is the issue of whether capitalism helps or hurts minorities. A third is the question whether different minorities respond differently to American capitalism.

I wrote a prelude scene for this story, one starring Shawnee's late mother. It centered on polio, and we learn that the father refused vaccines for the family because of the legacy of Tuskegee. Hence his guilt over Shawnee. I took it out because it imbalanced the immediate, MLK-centered story.

One concept mentioned by Shawnee is important for you to understand. The difference between mean and median can be crucial when looking at averages. The mean average is found by adding all numbers in the data set and then dividing by the number of values in the set.  The median is simply the middle value, when the set is arranged top to bottom. Always seek both.

Clearly, I have yet to plumb the depths of this story. I keep thinking about these characters. Shawnee and Saginaw Smith are apparently not done with me.

# Memphis ... was about unions and pay and working conditions, highlighting the problems of capitalism that have yet to be resolved.

## -- Douglas E. Thompson

GEOMETRY · GIRLS

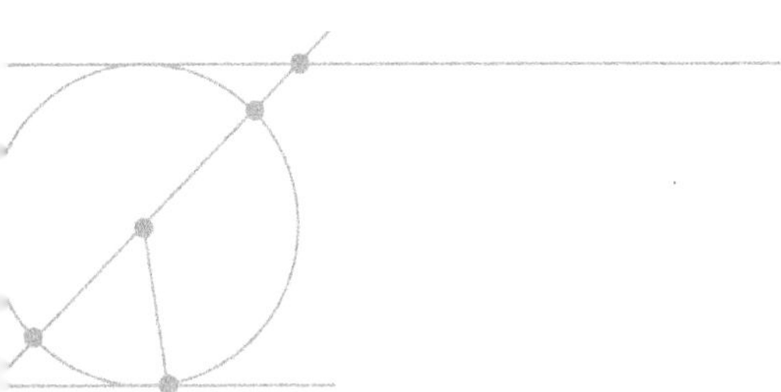

# BIOS

**Tom Durwood** is a teacher, writer and editor with an interest in history. Tom most recently taught English Composition and Empire and Literature at Valley Forge Military College, where he won the *Teacher of the Year* Award five times. Tom has taught Public Speaking and Basic Communications as guest lecturer for the Naval Special Warfare Development Group at the Dam's Neck Annex of the Naval War College.

Tom's ebook *Empire and Literature* matches global works of film and fiction to specific quadrants of empire, finding surprising parallels. Literature, film, art and architecture are viewed against the rise and fall of empire. In a foreword to *Empire and Literature*, postcolonial scholar Dipesh Chakrabarty of the University of Chicago calls it "imaginative and innovative." Prof. Chakrabarty writes that "Durwood has given us a thought-provoking introduction to the humanities." His subsequent book "Kid Lit: An Introduction to Literary Criticism" has been well-reviewed. "My favorite nonfiction book of the year," writes The Literary Apothecary (Goodreads).

Early reader response to Tom's historical fiction adventures has been promising. "A true pleasure ... the richness of the layers of Tom's novel is compelling," writes Fatima Sharrafedine in her foreword to "The Illustrated Boatman's Daughter." The Midwest Book Review calls that same adventure "uniformly gripping and educational ... pairing action and adventure with social issues." Adds Prairie Review, "A deeply intriguing, ambitious historical fiction series."

Tom briefly ran his own children's book imprint, Calico Books (Contemporary Books, Chicago). Tom's newspaper column "Shelter" appeared in the *North County Times* for seven years. Tom earned a Masters in English Literature in San Diego, where he also served as Executive Director of San Diego Habitat for Humanity.

Two of Tom's books, "Kid Lit" and "The Illustrated Boatman's Daughter," were selected "Best of the New" by Julie Sara Porter's *Bookworm Book* Alert 2021.

https://juliesaraporterbookworm.blogspot.com/2022/01/best-of-best-new-book-alert-2021.html?m=1

**Bonus: Tom interview:** https://www.circumlocution.net/2021/08/interview-with-thomas-durwood.html

**Sandra Uve**, author of "Superwomen, Superinventors: Brilliant Ideas that Transformed our Lives" has agreed to write a 400-word Foreword to *The Math Girls*.

An exhibit based on Sandra's book about female inventors from history has been shown at more than 200 libraries and museums such as Caixaforum Zaragoza, Palma, Girona, Tarragona and Lleida. The Commonwealth of Pamplona hosted  "Discovering Women Scientists" in 2021, and that same year, the *Gerència de Serveis de Biblioteques de la Diputació de Barcelona* produced an exhibition by Sandra, *Dones de la Mar*, about marine biologists and environmental activists.

**Mai Nguyen** is a rising illustrator of innovative work in concept art, animation and illustration. Mai studied in Singapore, where she discovered many types of art and animation. She now lives and works in Ho Chi Minh City. "The city is bursting with life and always vibrant. The chaos of a developing country means more opportunities, more corners to discover."

Mai's work also appears in Tom's ambitious trilogy set in the American Revolution, "The Illustrated Colonials."

*An example of Mai's animation work.*

# THE END

The **Science**  Girls

The **Aviation**  Girls

The **Zoology**  Girls

The **Botany** Girls

# Readers' comments on Tom's historical fiction

Exceedingly polished and well-crafted story. Meticulously researched ... complex and interesting.

-- Sarah Park Rankin, Common Threads

Luminous ... the story is encompassing, intelligent and layered.

-- Pharoah Miles, Graphic Policy Reviews

A work of great scope and adventure. The reach is far ...
An engaging series . . . We see the ripple effects of history.

-- Christopher Hoitash, author of "A Sister's Habit"

Wow ... unexpected. Skillful and entertaining.

-- Zara Miller, author of " I Am Cecilia"

*The Colonials* is clearly well-researched, containing the high-octane adventure
quotient of a James Michener novel and the imaginative complexity of a Harry Potter tale.

-- Marta Chang, Independent Book Reviews

Gorgeously written ... the author has done his research. The characters are clever, self-driven, and unique. These books are sure to spark curious minds.

-- Kerri Irish, ComfyReader book blog

Compelling ... surprising ... strong characterization ... a powerful draw.
Absorbing ... young readers of historical fiction will relish.

-- Diane Donovan, Midwest Book Review

Very literary, almost poetic writing and near flawless editing. I can see this book having wide-ranging appeal, not just teens, but also for adults as well. Highly recommended.

*-- Claire Middleton (Goodreads; Barnes & Noble; Indie Book Reviewers)*

Tom Durwood is the real thing.

*-- Joe Weber, Honorable Enemies, Rules of Engagement*

The debut of a wonderful writer ...

*-- Laraine Herring, Monsoons, Lost Fathers, and Lay My Sorrow Down*

A deeply intriguing, ambitious historical fiction series.

*-- Prairie Review*

# THE ADVENTURES OF RUBY PI AND THE GEOMETRY GIRLS

## BY TOM DURWOOD

Teen Heroines in History Use Geometry, Algebra and Other Mathematics to Solve Colossal Problems

FOREWORD BY SANDRA UVE

# The Adventures of Ruby Pi and the Geometry Girls

A robust entry into the YA field, this first "Ruby Pi" collection of adventures tells of brave heroines fighting tremendous odds, using the one tool that can save them – mathematics.

From ancient India to World War II, from Sputnik-era Moscow to the Benin Kingdoms and the Jim Crow South, clever girls overcome huge odds to save their families.

Few works of fiction truly transport the reader to another place and time, and even fewer give that reader something they can take back home afterwards. 'Geometry Girls' achieves both, breaking down barriers in educational literature and making mathematics not only interesting, but a matter of life and death. **Tom has done his homework ... this work will be a treasure of school libraries everywhere in years to come.**

**Written with a skillful hand** and with the kind of attention to detail that will grip an ambitious teenager.

The MLK story ... an excellent story with a crucially important message for young people in modern Western society. **The mathematics is simple but elegant.**

*-- Graham Van Goffrier, third-year PhD candidate (Theoretical neutrino physics)*

## www.themathgirls.com

STEM-BASED HISTORICAL FICTION

THE ADVENTURES OF
RUBY PI
AND THE
MATH GIRLS

BY TOM DURWOOD

Teen Heroines in History Use Geometry, Algebra and Other Mathematics to Solve Colossal Problems
FOREWORD BY SANDRA UVE

# The Adventures of Ruby Pi and the Math Girls

The second volume in this twin work, "The Adventures of Ruby Pi and the Math Girls" delivers five ambitious, not-for-everyone adventures to take young readers deep into mathematics and history. Our critical-thinking heroines are thrust into vivid settings from Mao's retreat to the cowboy West, from London to Palenque. Can they math their way out?

In this outstanding collection, Tom addresses the chronic problem of our young women dropping out of STEM studies. His stories lend adventure to scientific thinking.

"Sasha with the Red Hair" is thoughtful and surprising, like all Tom' s stories.

Exceptional ... a family drama disguised as an adventure.

-- *Tanzeela Siddique, Math Teacher*


# www.themathgirls.com

THE ILLUSTRATED COLONIAL

Home Fronts
Book Two

BY TOM DURWOOD

Durwood takes one of history's
greatest events and retells it through
these six wonderful, authentic, and
deeply relatable characters.
— Sara Ridley, Life of a Storyteller book blog

The meticulously rendered
illustrations ... shimmer
with depth and feeling.
— Prairies Book Review

# The Illustrated Colonials Trilogy

A new perspective one on of history's most fascinating moments. This richly illustrated trilogy captures some of the global thrill and tumult caused by the American
Revolution. The epic tale follows six young rich kids from around the world as they
join the cause, finding love and treachery along the path. Unique entry into the robust
YA universe.

A deeply intriguing, ambitious historical fiction series.

*-- Prairie Review*

Clever ....  Durwood's deeply realized characters are sketched with
precision and care.

*- Books Coffee Reviews*

## www.mycolonials.com

# The Illustrated Boatman's Daughter

An Egyptian girl fights intrigue and corruption for the completion of the world's greatest man-made waterway. Illustrated edition of a young-adult novella with 40 original color pieces. An attention-getting story featuring multicultural characters and settings. Classic adventure starring a smart, strong heroine.

"A true pleasure. The richness of the layers of Tom's novel is compelling."

*-- Fatima Sharrafedine, in her Foreword*

"Uniformly gripping and educational ... pairing action and adventure with social issues."

*--The Midwest Book Review*

## www.boatmansdaughter.com

ULYSSES S. GRANT IN CHINA
1879
THE ILLUSTRATED ULYSSES S. GRANT IN CHINA & other stories
BY TOM DURWOOD
ILLUSTRATED BY
Boell Oyino
Well-Bee
Sigurd Fernstrom

# The Illustrated 'Ulysses S. Grant in China' and Other Stories

Heroes coming of age... and changing history.

A lushly illustrated collection of stories from turning points in history, the adventures of brave teen protagonists trying desperately to meet the moment.

Poison and pistols, thieves and treachery, bandits and naval battles, opium dens and mysterious Caliphs and love triangles — readers will find it all in this colorful collection.

"All the makings of a wonderful literary property."

*-- Sherri Smith, Park Road Books*

www.usginchina.com

# HISTORICAL FICTION

# King James' Seventh Company

Yes, the obstacles are many, and time is short for the six young members of King James' Seventh Company. To save Six Companies of scholars, this fellowship of teenagers must cross a most dangerous landscape.

It begins as the simplest of stories: a young book-keeper (Matthias) is loaned out to one of his firm's clients. It seems there is some confusion in the client's ledgers. Matthias soon finds that the client is the King of England, and there is far more amiss in his kingdom than the ledgers. Dark and deadly forces swirl within Westminster Abbey, where the eminent scholars of the day are assembled to produce the world's greatest book: The King James Bible.

The novel's story-within-a-story is a sweeping account of Paul's real life, painting a very different portrait of the man who so effectively spread his version of Christianity.

Very literary, almost poetic writing and near flawless editing ... the author's narrative prose was some of the best and most authentic I've read in a while. (5 stars)

*-- Claire Middleton, Goodreads; Barnes & Noble; Indie Book Reviewers*

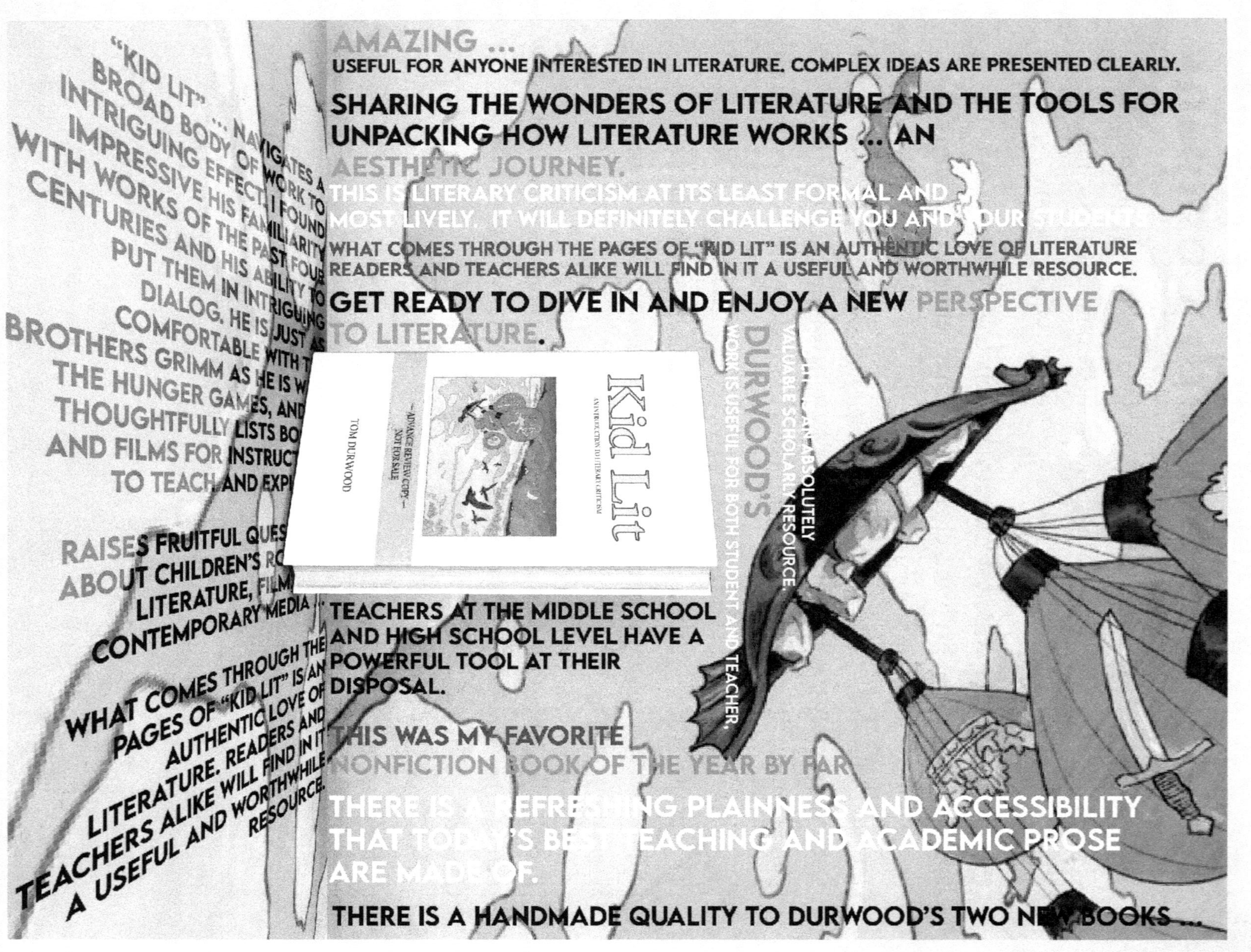
AMAZING …
USEFUL FOR ANYONE INTERESTED IN LITERATURE. COMPLEX IDEAS ARE PRESENTED CLEARLY.
SHARING THE WONDERS OF LITERATURE AND THE TOOLS FOR UNPACKING HOW LITERATURE WORKS … AN
AESTHETIC JOURNEY.
THIS IS LITERARY CRITICISM AT ITS LEAST FORMAL AND MOST LIVELY. IT WILL DEFINITELY CHALLENGE YOU AND YOUR STUDENTS.
WHAT COMES THROUGH THE PAGES OF "KID LIT" IS AN AUTHENTIC LOVE OF LITERATURE READERS AND TEACHERS ALIKE WILL FIND IN IT A USEFUL AND WORTHWHILE RESOURCE.
GET READY TO DIVE IN AND ENJOY A NEW PERSPECTIVE TO LITERATURE.
KID LIT IS AN ABSOLUTELY VALUABLE SCHOLARLY RESOURCE.
DURWOOD'S WORK IS USEFUL FOR BOTH STUDENT AND TEACHER,
"KID LIT" … NAVIGATES A BROAD BODY OF WORK TO INTRIGUING EFFECT. I FOUND IMPRESSIVE HIS FAMILIARITY WITH WORKS OF THE PAST FOUR CENTURIES AND HIS ABILITY TO PUT THEM IN INTRIGUING DIALOG. HE IS JUST AS COMFORTABLE WITH THE BROTHERS GRIMM AS HE IS WITH THE HUNGER GAMES, AND THOUGHTFULLY LISTS BOOKS AND FILMS FOR INSTRUCTORS TO TEACH AND EXPLORE.
RAISES FRUITFUL QUESTIONS ABOUT CHILDREN'S ROLE IN LITERATURE, FILM, CONTEMPORARY MEDIA
WHAT COMES THROUGH THE PAGES OF "KID LIT" IS AN AUTHENTIC LOVE OF LITERATURE. READERS AND TEACHERS ALIKE WILL FIND IN IT A USEFUL AND WORTHWHILE RESOURCE.
Kid Lit
AN INTRODUCTION TO LITERARY CRITICISM
— ADVANCE REVIEW COPY —
NOT FOR SALE
TOM DURWOOD
TEACHERS AT THE MIDDLE SCHOOL AND HIGH SCHOOL LEVEL HAVE A POWERFUL TOOL AT THEIR DISPOSAL.
THIS WAS MY FAVORITE NONFICTION BOOK OF THE YEAR BY FAR
THERE IS A REFRESHING PLAINNESS AND ACCESSIBILITY THAT TODAY'S BEST TEACHING AND ACADEMIC PROSE ARE MADE OF.
THERE IS A HANDMADE QUALITY TO DURWOOD'S TWO NEW BOOKS …

# Kid Lit: An Introduction to Literary Theory

There are twin premises to Tom Durwood's "Kid Lit: An Introduction to Literary Criticism."  The first is that literary theory is for all of us, and the second is that students can develop marketable lifetime skills when building critical thinking regarding their favorite stories.

Tom is a teacher and it is quickly evident in the clarity of his writing.  He poses a simple question – for example, *What makes a good villain?* -- and then draws you into a comparison between Captain Ahab (apocalyptic evil) and Dr. Octopus (simple greed). This then flows into a consideration of evil in all literature.  You are then invited to formulate your own theory of good and bad by following his clear illustrations.

**This is literary criticism at its least formal and most lively .... It will definitely challenge you and your students.**

-- Todd Whitaker, author of "What Great Teachers Do Differently"

My favorite non-fiction book of the year, by far.

-- The Literary Apothecary

# www.kidlitcrit.com

A STUDENT-FRIENDLY LENS
ON HUMANITIES

# Empire and Literature

## An Introduction

## Tom Durwood

FOREWORD BY DIPESH CHAKRABARTY

# Empire and Literature

Tom Durwood's supplemental-text e-book *Empire and Literature* promises to be an invaluable tool not only for students following his courses, but also for anyone interested to explore the deep relations between literature and empire.

Durwood brilliantly argues that literature and the workings of empire are deeply connected.

**An exceptional pedagogical tool, clear and concise exposition.**
*-- Andrei Ionescu, PhD in Languages/Literature and Psychology, University of Padua*

**Durwood has indeed given us a thought-provoking introduction to the humanities.** Teachers will find much here that is imaginative and innovative. I hope his book will receive the attention it deserves.
*-- Dipesh Chakrabarty, The University of Chicago, from his Foreword*

## www.empirestudies.com

A CASE STUDY IN NARRATIVE AND EMPIRE
TEDDY'S TANTRUM
JOHN D. WEAVER AND THE EXONERATION OF THE 25TH INFANTRY
TOM DURWOOD

# Teddy's Tantrum

*A Case Study in Empire and Literature*

This new account revisits a little-known 1906 incident in Teddy Roosevelt's administration and finds an epic "lost" story of intrigue, combat, politics and redemption.

On November 5, 1906, Roosevelt dismissed 167 members of the 25th Infantry in what historian Lewis Gould calls "one of the most glaring miscarriages of justice in American history."

Sixty years later, a journeyman writer named John D. Weaver, the son of a clerk at the 1906 hearings, embarked on a campaign to exonerate the soldiers. His book produced a small measure of justice: in February of 1973, the U.S. Army issued an apology to the men of the 25th Infantry and awarded the sole surviving battalion member (Dorsie Willis) back pay.

This is the first chronicle of the entire Brownsville story, treating Weaver and the troops' exoneration as an equal part of the narrative. Author Tom Durwood scratches the surface of "Teddy's tantrum" and finds a confluence of rich characters and enduring themes. It is a story of military heroism and redemption, loyalty and betrayal, presidential influence and the power of narrative. *Teddy's Tantrum* seeks to set the neglected episode in its historical context.

'Teddy's Tantrum' takes a period of history and shines new light on it ... Tom pulls out the grander themes of the tragedy and triumph. The true stuff of history.

*-- Tim Pritchard, author "Ambush Alley"*

www.teddystantrum.com

# Ruby Pi and the Botany Girls

Smart and resourceful girls coming of age star in unexpected scenarios from our rich history with the plant world

This time, Ruby and her fellow heroines take on the plant kingdom and emerge with out-of-ordinary adventures and science-based resolutions.  First, Ruby is drawn into an international drama while engineering a new wing of Kew Gardens. Tea plantations and poppy-field rivalries mix with the India independence movement to create a witches' brew for Rupa and her family.

In other times and places, we meet teen seed-hunters in Tibet;  a young novitiate helping Gregor Mendel make sense of his experiments in genetics;  a young police detective in Mexico City and his botanist sister as they fight powerful forces in a deadly intrigue over Norman Borlaug's Green Revolution on the plains of Queretaro. The Irish potato famine threatens young Marcy and her extended clan. The sudden failure of a corn crop triggers the fall of Palenque. The 'Botany Girls' collection ends with a science fiction drama regarding the future of botany.

# www.themathgirls.com